BATTERED NOT Broken

Gillian Locke has been beaten, battered, and bruised, but her ex-boyfriend still hasn't managed to break her. When she leaves Kyle for the last time, she knows the only way she'll ever be back in his grasp is over her dead body.

On the run, her car disastrously breaks down in at the top of a mountain in the middle of nowhere. Stuck in a terrible snowstorm, Gillian figures it's better to die at the hands of nature, than at the hands of Kyle, her tormentor. Fighting the freezing cold, she stares death in the eye and presses on, until she happens upon a cabin in the woods, and is offered shelter by three gorgeous men who can't seem to get enough of her.

The Bearclaw brothers are descendants of the ancient Anikota tribe of Indians. Their beast spirit and blessing from the Maker allows them the ability to sense the one who will complete their soul. Being triplets, they always expected their mate to be a woman they'd all share. With the Maker's blessing, they hope to ease past Gillian's defenses…before her past threatens to end their future.

Chapter One

Sleet whipped through the trees, stinging her face and burrowing through her clothes to chill her skin. Gillian tightened her hold on the jacket as the wind threatened to yank it from her shoulders. Her fingers tunneled into her skimpy pockets, searching for warmth that wasn't there. Feet crunching and sinking into the dangerous snow brought her closer and closer to her goal. Warmth was only footsteps away…many, many footsteps.

From the road, where she'd left her broken-down car, the smoke rising in the trees hadn't seemed too far off. Now, hours later, it seemed like she'd been walking for an eternity. Gillian was tempted to check her watch again, to see how long she'd been walking down the slushy, rutted road, but couldn't force her hands to leave the haven in her pockets.

One foot in front of the other, she kept trekking, stumbling over unseen rocks and tripping in hidden holes. Exhaustion began to overtake her. Each breath puffed from her mouth, turning the air bright white before she sucked back in frigid air, which seemed to freeze Gillian from the inside out. But she couldn't stop, could never stop.

The worn road she followed twisted and turned through the trees. Every time she came to a bend, she made a wish that her destination would be around the next corner. But it wasn't, so she kept pushing, begging her feet to move.

Mind over matter, girl, just a few more steps.

She'd lost the feeling in her feet hours before. The wind picked up again and pummeled the sleet into her skin like a thousand tiny knives. Hunching her shoulders to shield her face, she continued.

Can't stop. He'll catch me.

She couldn't afford to get caught. She wouldn't go back, not ever again. The last time…the last time she'd nearly died. Not again, not ever again.

Gillian licked her lips, tasting blood as her tongue wet her cracked skin. Hours. It had only taken hours for the cold and wind to do its damage.

Tears pricked her eyes and more than once she thought about returning to her car to wait for someone to pass by, to help her. But on these deserted mountain roads, hardly anyone ever drove by, especially with a blizzard churning and threatening the area. Now she would die in the cold, alone.

At least it would happen her way and not at another's hands.

More time passed and each breath became more labored—the only sound the harsh inhalation and exhalation as she tried to fill her lungs. The landscape was bare of animals, not even the squawk of a bird could be heard to distract her from the struggle to keep going. They were probably snuggled in their own homes for the winter.

Smart bastards.

Shadows crossed the road now, the sun having dipped behind the trees for its own slumber. The smoke had looked so close when she started out; she should have known. Gillian wasn't an outdoorsy woman—close to her, ended up being miles and miles away in reality. But still she continued. She'd walk until she collapsed or found warmth for the night; whichever came first.

Head down, she lumbered on. It wasn't until she ran into the gate that she realized she'd reached her destination. The end of the road had come and now she stood before what she'd been dreaming of all day.

A cottage. No, a cabin. A large log cabin with wisps of smoke wafting from the chimney proved she hadn't been walking toward a dream. With weathered logs forming the walls and a wood shingle roof, it looked like a solid structure, built to spite the elements.

She tugged her hand free of her coat pocket and lifted the latch on the gate, calling out a greeting as she stepped through the wooden portal.

"Hello?"

Her voice was lost with the wind and pain sliced through her throat. The damaged tissues still hadn't healed.

Closing the gate behind her and dropping the latch in place to make sure it was locked, she stepped across the snow-covered lawn. Careful of any hidden dangers, she tested the ground with each step just as she'd done all day. She didn't want to stumble and fall when so close to her goal. Sheer determination kept her on her feet now, denying the toll the weather had taken on her body.

One puffing breath and straining step at a time she climbed the steps, shuffling across the worn plank porch to the front door. She'd burrowed her hand back in the meager warmth in her pocket, but she reluctantly withdrew it again. Raising the knocker, she let it fall against the tarnished brass plate on the door, its booming echo mixing with the wind as it whipped around the cabin. *All that, for nothing.*

Gillian waited, but no sound from within the cabin could be heard. She forced her muscles into action again, raising and releasing the knocker to fall against the brass plate for a second time. The sound echoed, louder this time, yet still there was no answer.

Tears burned her eyes, and she didn't hold them back. A fire burned in their hearth and they were either not home or choosing to ignore the bundled, bruised, and beaten woman at their door.

Gillian rest her head against the carved wooden door and she let her tears flow, the warm liquid stinging her near frozen skin as it slid across her cheeks. In a last effort for survival and with the remaining strength she possessed, Gillian wrapped her hand around the doorknob and twisted, stumbling when the door pushed open with her weight.

She caught herself on the door then stepped into the cabin. Warmth like she never thought to feel again enveloped her, seeped through her jeans and poor excuse for a jacket. As the heat surrounded her body, pinpricks of pain replaced the numbness she had grown accustomed to. Her waking skin burned as blood returned to her extremities.

She leaned against the door, pushing it closed to stop any more of the luxurious heat from leaving the cabin. Her breath still came in soft pants and Gillian swallowed, wincing at the pain the action caused.

Damn him!

She wet her lips, then called out to the cabin's inhabitants again, hoping now they would hear her.

"Hello?" she croaked. Her voice didn't resemble the soft timber she normally had. Damn Kyle to the farthest reaches of hell.

Seconds ticked by as she waited, frozen to the spot, her clothes dripping water and mud on the mat in front of the door. No one answered. A clock chimed from within the cabin. Seven o'clock. She'd been trudging through the woods for thirteen hours and been awake for thirty-five. Acknowledging the amount of time she'd been awake only managed to make her fatigue intensify.

Gillian moved a few steps into the cabin and spotted the source of all the glorious heat—a fire roaring away behind the hearth screen.

She croaked out another greeting. "Hello?"

She tried raising her voice, but it only cracked and pain knifed down her throat. Gillian swallowed hard in a vain effort to relieve the pain and shuffled forward a few more steps, knocking on the worn plank wall to rouse the cabin's inhabitants.

Still no one replied. Could the house be empty?

She shuffled further into the cabin, her eyes drinking in the home's interior. Large, wood-framed couches lined the living room's walls, and an enormous rug covered the floor with a tree stump coffee table in the center. It emitted a sense of warmth and welcome, with throw blankets covering the couch and handmade end tables capping each couch. Cozy.

Gillian continued through the cabin, praying the owners wouldn't throw her out or be angry for entering without an invitation. She passed by a tidy, but small kitchen; a carved table occupied the center of the space. She kept moving through the cabin until she came upon five doors.

The first opened into a spacious bathroom with four sinks, a massive tub and a walk-in shower. The door closed with a soft click, and Gillian moved on to the door directly across the hall.

Gillian peered inside to find clothes strewn all over the room, soda cans sitting on the dresser, and shoes littering the floor. This was, without a doubt, a man's room. A messy man, but a man nonetheless. Slob or not, at least *someone* lived in the house; there was no way she would have dreamed up that mess.

The heat and movement wakened her limbs as she moved on to the next room, and her cold aches were swiftly becoming definite pain. The wide open door revealed a tidy yet lived-in room. Pictures lined the walls and the bed appeared to have been made with care, the top blanket pulled taut along the mattress.

Fatigue wore on her and Gillian hoped she either came upon a guest room or one of the cabin's occupants soon. She felt as if she'd drop to the ground if she didn't get off of her feet.

The last door—Gillian peered inside to find a sparsely furnished room. A full-sized bed covered with a plain comforter in one corner, the small bedside table right beside it holding a single lamp. There were no pictures on the walls; nothing at all to show the room belonged to someone. *Must be the guest room.*

Her shoes clopped against the wooden floor as she trod across the room, before settling on the bed. She toed her shoes off and pain shot into her legs at the movement. There was nothing she could do about that now; the damage had been done. Gillian swung her legs onto the bed and laid her head on the pillow, pulling the blanket across the bed and over her body. Tucked into the warmth of the comforter, Gillian allowed the quiet ticking of the house's clock lull her to sleep. She'd explain her presence to the cabin's owners, but right now, she just needed to rest her eyes. Just…for…a…minute.

* * *

Ronan stomped through the snow toward his brothers, not quite ready to head back toward home. They didn't seem to be too worried about heading back to the cabin either. Conner took strikes at Max, swiping and clawing at his brother while Max jumped and jogged out of Conner's way.

Ronan lumbered through the melting snow shaking off the growing layer of frosty ice and leaned against a nearby tree, rubbing his back against the bark. He stretched tall, then pressed against the tree with his front legs above his head, gouging the tree and marking his territory. An Alpha bear had to make his space known and being the biggest, strongest and oldest bears in the region, Ronan didn't want anyone but he and his brothers in the area.

The growls from Conner and Max grew louder, drawing his attention away from his task. Max, being the bigger of the two, pinned Conner to the ground and held him with his razor-sharp teeth, clutching his throat. Conner continued to struggle and swipe at Max, but Max didn't look as if he would release him anytime soon.

Dropping to all fours, Ronan loped toward the two bears. Several feet from them, he growled low, but steady, showing his displeasure. Max's eye met his for a moment before he released Conner with a snort. Sometimes, just sometimes, the bear took too much control and animal instinct overrode their human emotions.

Most confrontations between bears were one-on-one. With a third left out of the fight, there would always be someone around to break it up. That's what made their brotherly triad work.

Ronan shook his head at the two of them then turned and started for home. Darkness would be upon them soon and the fire he'd started before leaving the cabin beckoned him. The sounds of Conner and Max following in his footsteps met his ears and he was pleased they'd decided to follow. While he couldn't force them to head home with him, he always enjoyed their company.

As they trudged through the forest's undergrowth, Ronan used his body to push bushes and branches out of his way, his fur-encased feet sloshing in the wet snow. The falling snow turned to sleet and coated his fur and he was thankful for the insulation his bear form provided from the elements. His breath turned white as it met the frigid air and he didn't look forward to changing back to his naked human form on the back porch of their cabin. *No bears in the house.* That was their rule. It had actually been their mother's rule, but they had kept it in place even if she did live on the other side of the country.

The scent of his fire and the plume of smoke rising above the trees guided him home. As he approached the back porch he shook off the excess snow and moisture before making his way up the steel reinforced steps and then waited for his brothers to join him.

They formed their sacred triangle and recited the ancient words calling upon the Maker to assist in their change from beast to man. As one, the mists rose and enveloped their bestial bodies and flowed into their noses and mouths to touch their souls. Bones cracked while muscles retracted and shifted, changing them from bear to mirror images of each other. In seconds, with no hint of pain, men stood where bears once did. The moment the transformation was complete, the mystical ancient mist returned to its place within the earth, leaving them naked and cold.

Without waiting for his brothers, Ronan dashed for the back door and darted toward the living room. Snatching his sweatpants from the couch, he yanked them on and then wrapped a blanket around his shoulder before flopping onto the worn sofa. The worst part of shifting from beast to man in the dead of winter? The cold. It was enough to make his balls hibernate in his chest for the season. Goose-bumps lined his skin as he shook, slumped on the couch letting the warmth from the fire seep into his body. *Heaven.*

Conner and Max were quick to follow, both of them going through the same motions he just had. When they had all settled on the couch before the roaring hearth, Ronan relaxed into the cushions.

The scents of home teased his nostrils—a mix of burning wood, his brothers' musk, and cinnamon permeated the entire cabin. But he sensed something else, something different, new…feminine? *No*. No woman lived on the mountain. The closest woman was the forest ranger, and she lived at least twenty miles away, in town. He must be just catching her leftover scent from her last visit. But it didn't smell like her. It smelled like vanilla and lavender, with just a hint of mint. So sweet. Intoxicating. Raising his head off the couch, Ronan looked at Conner and Max. They both held the same expression of confusion he was sure he wore. Did they smell the fragrance too?

Rising from the couch, Ronan tightened the blanket around his shoulders, hesitant to lose the warmth he'd acquired. He paused near the living room entrance as something on the floor caught his eye. Muddy footprints marred his perfectly polished wood floors. Mud! The perpetrator was a dead man walking. When he glanced over his shoulder he saw Conner and Max had risen to follow him. Ronan pressed his finger to his lips, motioning for them to remain silent.

Ronan followed the prints through their home, cringing with each step as he saw more and more mud and melted snow defacing his beautiful floors. The hint of scent he'd caught in the living room grew stronger as he traveled down the hall.

They seemed to travel from room to room, stopping first at the bathroom, and then traveling to Max's bedroom, before moving to Conner's and finally entering his. His room. The owner of the addictive scent and muddy feet quite possibly resided on the other side of *his* closed bedroom door.

The muddy footprints disappeared beneath his door. Not only did the owner of the lovely scent teasing his nostrils reside on the other side of the inch of wood, so did the owner of the muddy marks.

The two halves of his being warred within; the human side, holding steadfast to his fastidious nature, raged at the dirt, snow and mud traipsed through his home. Meanwhile, his beast roared in triumph over finding its mate.

Its mate? No. His beast was just hungry. After all, they'd been out into the snow-laden forest and hadn't hunted while they were out. His mate couldn't be on the other side of the door, could she?

"Ronan?"

Max growled at him. Growled! His gaze shifted to his brother and he found a look which surely mirrored his own. Lust, hunger, and need flashed across Max's face. One look at Conner, and he saw the same.

His voice just a whisper, he addressed his brothers.

"We don't touch her. We'll talk about it after we figure out who she is, and why she's here. For now, we keep our distance until we know more, agreed?"

They replied in unison through gritted, grinding teeth.

"Agreed."

Ronan turned the knob and pushed open the door on its silent hinges and stared at the beauty…and she was filthy…and, goddamn it, in his bed!

Chapter Two

Gillian wasn't sure what woke her. One moment she lazed in a blissful, dreamless sleep and the next her body jerked, muscles tensing as her eyes shot open. Sleep blurred her vision, but her ears picked up deep, baritone voices while her eyes discerned three large shapes near the bed.

He'd found her. Her heart sank, and her fear rose. *So quick, how did he always seem to be so quick?* They hadn't seemed to have noticed she had awoken, they continued their argument. With small, snakelike movements, she inched her way to the opposite side of the bed, their voices still low and angry.

She blinked to clear the sleepy haze of her vision, and focused on three identical men standing in a circle mere feet from where she lay.

Ohshitohfuckohshitohfuck!

They stood, albeit preoccupied, between her and freedom. Her muscles ached and stung, making their protest known as she covertly shifted and squirmed to the opposite side of the bed, placing as much space as she could between her and them. She kept her attention focused on the men as she moved. She reached the edge of the bed, but just as she was about to tip over the edge and drop to the floor, one of the men noticed her.

"Hey! She's awake!" The man on the left elbowed the man in the middle.

Three sets of crystal blue eyes swung to meet hers. Without thought she dropped to the ground beside the bed, grunting when her feet screamed in protest. She couldn't think about pain now. Kyle had sent them to take her back. He was probably nearby and the moment he got his hands on her, she'd be dead. But she'd die fighting them before she gave Kyle the satisfaction of killing her.

Gillian's eyes darted around the room, searching for a weapon, but none lay within reach. Staying in a low crouch, her back struck the wall as she tried to put more distance between her and the men. Her heart hammered her chest while her breath came in great bellows. A panic attack loomed on the horizon, but she couldn't let her panic overtake her, she needed to remain calm; hyperventilating wouldn't get her out of this mess.

Staying low, she eased to the foot of the bed, but the men kept their distance. It was now or never. Gillian gathered her remaining strength then darted for the open door. She made it to the doorway before muscled arms wrapped around her waist, halting her escape.

Tears poured down her face as she hammered at her captor, struggling to free herself, but it was no use, his grip was like iron. The men's voices raised, but she couldn't understand what they were saying over the roar of her own heartbeat echoing in her ears.

I don't want to die. I don't want to die. I don't want to die.

Another set of arms scooped her away from her captor and the room fell silent. A few whispered words made it through, halting her struggles.

"You're not going to die, poppet. We'll protect you. No one here will hurt you, ever."

The man who cradled her in his arms sat on the bed, placing her in his lap with care. Her heart raced and her breath came in frightened pants as two sets of blue eyes bore into her. One of the men reached toward her and she flinched on instinct.

Gillian swallowed hard, wincing with the pain that remained. "I'm sorry I broke into your house. I'll just get my shoes…" She tried to wiggle free of the man's grasp.

"You're not going anywhere," the man in front of her growled.

The man holding her tightened his arms around her and growled back at the one before her. "Ronan. If you can't stay calm, leave. Better yet, why don't you both leave? Max, take Ronan out of here."

The man she now knew as Max tugged on Ronan's sleeve and they both backed out of the room, leaving her alone with the man whose name she still didn't know.

He slid her off his lap and onto the bed, before dropping to his knees on the floor in front of her. His hand approached her face and she flinched again. She snapped her eyes shut and waited for the hit to come, but it didn't. *Why hadn't he just hit her already?*

Opening her eyes, she found him staring at her, mouth hanging agape, eyes wide. He eased back, putting more space between them before he spoke. His hands rested on the bed, one on each side of her hips.

"My name's Conner. We're not mad you broke in. Why don't you tell me your name?" Conner's voice was deep, soft, soothing her nerves and calming her heart as he spoke. *Was he lulling her into submission before he pounced?*

"Gillian." Her throat, still raw from Kyle's most recent attack, ached.

"Gillian." His eyes flicked down her legs and she was reminded of the throbbing pain in her feet. "You're hurt, Gillian."

Adrenaline had kept the aches at bay, but they were slowly returning with full force. Her ankles, feet and toes were covered in blisters and raw spots. Some of them oozed blood, staining the carpet and smearing on the floor.

"Oh, God. I'm so sorry. I didn't mean… I'll just clean up this mess and get out of your way. I'm so sorry." She was babbling, she knew it, but couldn't stop.

Gillian reached for her snow-soaked shoes and socks and saw what she'd missed when she kicked them off before climbing into bed. Amidst the mud stains were dark splotches of red—blood red. The cold had deadened her nerves, making her poor feet numb and they'd paid the price. Her feet throbbed at the thought of putting the shoes back on. Conner's warm hands wrapped around hers, and before she could snatch them away, he placed her hands on her thighs and released her.

"We'd like you to stay. You're obviously hurt. There wasn't a car parked out front when we came home and it's obvious you walked and we can't, in good conscience, let you go back out in that weather. You're welcome to stay here, Gillian."

Gillian twined her fingers as she thought about her options. Honestly? There weren't any options. It wasn't like she was in any condition to walk and her car had died along the road. If these three weren't after her she now had to worry about them, too. If she stayed like Connor asked, what would Kyle do to them when he found her? It was no longer a question of if, but when.

"But I'm a stranger to you. Your brother, Ronan, didn't seem too thrilled with me…"

His warm hands enveloped hers and Gillian's gaze traveled up his toned honey-tinted arms across his broad shoulders and came to rest on Conner's face. Kind eyes bored into hers and she felt as if she could get lost in them forever.

"Believe me, Ronan doesn't want you back out there any more than I do. Besides, we're three men living in the middle of nowhere with only each other for company. It'll be a pleasure to have someone to talk to." Conner gave her a small smile, a simple tilting of his lips, barely revealing his bright white teeth.

"You're sure?" Gillian hated taking advantage of the brothers' hospitality, but she couldn't afford to turn it down, not with her feet shredded the way they were and her car not operating. She wouldn't stay long, but she couldn't run without getting some rest. She'd stay a day, two tops. Just spend some time recovering.

"I'm more than sure." Conner unfolded his body from the floor in one fluid movement. Gillian followed his progress with her eyes and was amazed at how tall he was. Sitting on the bed as she was, Conner towered above her. "Now, how about a bath? Or a shower?"

Gillian looked over her clothes. Mud had spattered all over her clothes and still clung to the bottom of her jeans. She couldn't even begin to imagine what the rest of her looked like now. Normally her hair hung in beautiful ringlets, but she was sure that by now they frizzed in every direction. A soak in a tub sounded divine, but there was no way she could lower her body into a big 'ole tub of water and crawl out again. At best, she thought she could sit on the shower floor as the water poured over her.

"Shower. A shower sounds good; I can just sit on the floor. Ya know, considering." She wiggled her feet to get her point across.

"No worries. We've got a shower that will take your breath away." He bent down to her eye level, the same smile playing on his lips. "I'm going to lift you up and carry you to the bathroom, is that okay? Don't want you injuring yourself more than you already have."

Nodding, she was swept into Conner's arms before she had a chance to say "okay". Gillian let out a screech as she wrapped her arms around his neck and held on tight.

He strode toward the door with Gillian holding on for dear life. Feet from the door, it swung open and Gillian stared into Max and Ronan's eyes. She couldn't tell them apart, but one of them barked a question at Conner.

"Well?" *That must be Ronan.*

"She's staying with us for now. Back up, will ya? I'm taking her to the bathroom and I can't get there with you two standing in the way."

Both men backed down the hall, grumbling while never taking their eyes off her. Maybe Conner had been lying when he said she'd be welcome. She couldn't read the looks on Max and Ronan's faces, but they definitely didn't say, 'Welcome!'

Max swung the bathroom door open and stood back. His hand held Ronan's wrist, seeming to hold him back as well. Conner kept his steps even and firm as he made his way into the bathroom. Turning sideways, he moved into the room with ease. Gillian was surprised when he kicked the door shut with his heel, keeping Max and Ronan out, but also closing them in the room together.

This was it. The other shoe was falling in the form of Conner being a total pervert and forcing her to take a shower while he watched—or worse, participated.

Conner knocked the lid to the toilet seat down before seating her on it. He left her there and went around the corner to what Gillian presumed was the linen closet and came back carrying a fluffy robe and towel.

"So, we've got the fluffy robe, a towel, and a washcloth. I also grabbed an extra towel to dry off with for later."

"Why two towels?"

A pale blush stained Conner's sun-kissed face before he answered. "Well, I figured you could get undressed and wrap this one around you while I carried you into the shower. The second one is to dry off later. The shower is huge, with adjustable showerheads and a bench seat. We can get everything angled just right for you before I leave and then you won't have to stand to shower. It's not ideal…"

"It's perfect."

She earned a blinding smile from Conner as he rubbed his hands on his jeans.

Twice in fifteen minutes Conner had proven he wasn't anything like Kyle. She would have earned a smack for smearing blood on the floor, even if he had been the cause. And not once had Kyle ever thought about her comfort or privacy. It was always about what made Kyle happy.

"I'll just stand over here, with my back turned of course, while you get undressed. Yell when you're ready."

Gillian waited until Conner disappeared around the corner then began peeling her layers from her body. First her jacket, then her sweatshirt, and finally her t-shirt, leaving her in her bra covering her breasts. Free of her clothes, the scent of sweat and mud hit her like a ton of bricks. *Ew!* Body odor did not even begin to describe her scent. How had Conner not wrinkled his nose at the thought of carrying her? She smelled ripe!

Gillian flicked open the button on her jeans, lowered the zipper and began her own version of a caterpillar wiggle to get her jeans past her hips without standing. By the time she got them down to her thighs, she panted from the exertion. The soaked and soiled garment made a splat when she dropped it onto her growing pile of clothing.

She looked around the bathroom to make sure Conner was still out of eyesight. He was, so Gillian repeated her caterpillar wiggle to remove her panties, draping the towel over her lap just in case Conner didn't hold to his word. She held one side pressed between her chin and chest as she reached behind her to unlatch her bra. She added it to her pile of laundry before wrapping the towel firmly around her chest and making sure her lower body was covered. Happy she was as covered as she could be, she yelled—well, croaked—for Conner.

"Conner?"

He appeared from around the corner. His pale blush had deepened to a fire engine red. "All set?"

"As I'll ever be." Gillian mustered the best smile she could, but inside she quaked like a leaf. Conner came to her side and scooped her into his arms without any apparent effort, but this time, she kept her hands to herself. The last thing she wanted to do was flash the man. The situation was awkward enough.

He carried her around the corner where he had been waiting and she got a good look at the shower she had only glanced at before. Massive didn't begin to describe the glass enclosure. The bottom half of the walk-in shower was what appeared to be a marble wall while the top half consisted of large panes of glass. The door, also glass, was propped open and Conner carried her into the shower and settled her onto a built-in bench.

The shower *room* is what he should have called it. The space looked as if it could easily fit three or more people. There were showerheads in so many different places Gillian didn't think she could count them all. Preoccupied with her surroundings, she'd completely forgotten Conner was with her. Well, until he plopped down onto the bench beside her. She let out a squeak of surprise.

He held out some sort of wireless computer panel. Taking it in her hands, she stared at him.

"And I'm doing what with this exactly?"

"That controls all of the showerheads in here. All you have to do is pick one and a directional screen comes up and you can move it around until you like where it's at. Then push 'OK'. We each have our own settings pre-programmed, but we can program one for you while you're here so you don't have to mess with it so much every time you shower."

She needed to cut him off at the pass. If she stayed too long, Kyle would surely find her. "I'm not going to be here very long. You don't have to program anything for me."

"Oh, it's no trouble."

Conner took the computer panel back from her and messed with a few showerheads until he seemed happy with the array. "How hot do you like it? Lukewarm, skin burning, or somewhere in between."

"In between." She wasn't going to fight with the man if he wanted to program the stupid machine. It was his toy.

"Girl after my own heart." Conner winked at her before returning his attention to the panel and butterflies seemed to take up residence in her belly. Where was pesticide when she needed some? Gillian didn't need to crush on some guy while she was running from Kyle. Getting tangled up with a man while on the run wouldn't be a good idea. He'd try to convince her he could take care of anything and damn if she wouldn't be tempted to believe him.

When everything was settled to his liking, he rose from the bench. "Well, push this button here and the water starts collecting in the reservoir from the water heater. When it's gathered enough of the water at the right temperature, it'll come out of the showerheads, but not before it gives you a ten second warning."

"Okay." She nodded.

"Great! I'll leave your other towel near the door. You should be able to reach it, but it won't get wet. When you're done and ready for me to come get you, just push the intercom button and speak. I'll hear you no matter what."

"Okay." Her smell was getting to her, how could he stand to be so close and in such a confined space with her?

With a nod of his head Conner turned and was steps away from the shower door when Gillian called him back.

"Conner!" When he turned to face her, she felt those damn butterflies flutter and bounce again. *Stupid things.*

"I just…I just want to…" Tears were forming in her eyes, but she refused to cry in front of a near stranger. They could wait until she was snuggled in bed, alone. "I just want to thank you, for everything."

"It's my pleasure, Gillian."

He turned away from her again and she yelled one last request. Well, croaked it at least.

"Can you thank your brothers too? Tell them I'm sorry for making such a mess and…well, for everything."

"It's no problem, Gillian. We're happy to have you here. Now, enjoy your shower and just give a yell when you're done."

Chapter Three

When he stepped into the hall, Conner noticed Ronan's handiwork right away—every trace of the mud and blood Gillian tracked through the cabin had been wiped clean. Their home appeared spotless once again.

Conner padded down the hall and he found his brothers just where he thought they'd be, pacing the living room and snarling at one another. The tension would only rise when he told them what he'd seen on Gillian.

Ronan noticed his presence first and stomped to stand before him.

"Well?" Did the man ever talk instead of growl or bark?

"She's taking a shower…"

"You saw her naked? Shit. Lucky bastard." Damn, Max's mind was always on one thing.

"No, I did not see her naked. I gave her privacy, which she deserves. Sit down, both of you."

"Why?"

"Just sit down, Ronan."

They grumbled while they did it, but Conner's brothers did as he asked. Thank God! He wasn't sure where to start explaining what he'd seen and surmised from his time with Gillian, but they didn't give him much time to think. They wanted answers, now. The moment Ronan's backside touched the couch, his questions began.

"Well? Is she staying? Of course she's staying. You didn't give her a choice, right?" Ronan pointed at him. "Right?"

"Yes, she's staying, but I gave her a choice, Ronan. We can't kidnap her. I have a feeling she's been manhandled enough." He pointed a finger at Ronan, making sure his brother was paying attention. "You need to cool it with the caveman act. You scared her witless." Conner couldn't sit any longer, he stood and began pacing. "I'm pretty sure she's been abused by a man. Why do you think she mumbled she didn't want to die? I think dying by a man's hands was a real possibility for her not too long ago."

His statement got Max's attention and both of his brothers leaned forward, resting their elbows on their knees, eyes narrowed.

"What do you mean?" The menace in Max's voice was unmistakable. Ronan may rant and rave, but deep down, he was fair and level headed. Max, well, Max just wasn't. "Gillian has bruising around her throat, four fingers and a thumb spanning her neck, and the same on her arms. I think she's running from someone, and I don't doubt she only plans to stay for a couple of days until her feet are healed enough to walk. Then she'll be gone again."

Ronan's denial was instantaneous. "No."

Conner ran his hands through his hair, and then slid his hands down to his neck, rubbing and kneading the tense muscles.

"I know, Ronan, I know." Conner stated the obvious as he looked at his two brothers. "Look, she's here now. We need to make her feel comfortable and safe. We'll give her the room across from yours, Ronan. But you guys better not try paying her any late night visits. Understood?"

Ronan jerked his head in a brisk nod, but Max's gaze was unfocused at the wall behind him.

"Max?"

"Someone hurt her, Conner, and I want to know who."

Damn Max and their mother's teachings.

"I know, Max, but I didn't even ask her about the bruises. She's upset. I didn't want to upset her further. I was only trying to get her into the shower and cleaned up."

Sighing, Conner flopped back onto the couch. Gillian had been in their lives for barely half an hour yet the emotional connection already felt stronger than a mere acquaintance. He was sure Max and Ronan were having the same feelings toward her as he was. His bear wanted to hunt down and kill the man who dared to harm his mate, their mate. Gillian's scent identified her as their bears' mate and she would be the center of their triad and complete their souls.

A hesitant, croaking voice interrupted their conversation.

"Conner?"

All three men's bodies jerked at the sound. Max rose from the couch and moved toward the kitchen, yelling an order over his shoulder.

"Conner, let her know you'll be a minute."

"Why?"

"I'm going to grab some salves for her wounds and then I'll go take care of her."

Conner and Ronan jumped from the couch to follow Max.

"Do you think that's wise? I mean, she seems comfortable with me…" The truth of it was, Conner wanted to catch another glimpse of a half-clothed Gillian.

Max stopped his search in the pantry and faced him. "She needs to be comfortable with all of us, Conner. I am the most medically inclined out of the three of us, right?"

"Well, yeah."

"So, I'm going to tend her wounds. I'm not going to molest her or force her to do anything, but I am going to take care of her."

Max returned his attention to gathering the jars and bandages he needed, leaving Conner to stare at his brother's back.

"Why don't you and Ronan see about dinner while I take care of our Gilly?"

With that, Max, clutching his jars of medicines and bandages disappeared down the hall.

*

Max was thankful for the bottles and bandages in his hands, they masked the fact that his hands shook and twitched. Anger of the likes he'd never known coursed through his blood, pushing it closer to boiling with every step he took.

Max stood outside the bathroom door, pausing for a moment as he took a deep breath, releasing it slowly through his mouth. Anger and nervous tension buzzed through his body now. He needed to do his best to balance the anger of the beast and the nervousness of the man while he spoke with and tended Gillian. Too much of either would definitely scare her and push her away from him, and them.

Twisting the knob with care, he nudged the door open and stepped into the steam-filled bathroom. The increasingly familiar scents of vanilla, lavender and mint assaulted his senses, but now there was the added scent of his favorite shampoo.

Max called out Gillian's name, alerting her to his presence.

"Gillian?"

"I'm still in the shower… I had a bit of trouble and…"

Her voice trailed off to a quiet mumble he couldn't quite make out. When he turned the corner, he saw her problem immediately. She had managed to drape the towel around her, but couldn't quite get it beneath her rear end, leaving that bit of pale, delicate flesh exposed.

His eyes swallowed her body whole. Max hadn't managed to get more than a glimpse of her tiny form when she lay in Ronan's bed, but now he had the opportunity to see her—all of her. From her water-soaked golden ringlets to her buttermilk skin and luscious curves, Max could see it all. Her pale brown eyes locked with his and a light blush dusted her cheeks before she looked away.

Damn, he needed to get a hold of his lust and rein it in. His cock was way too interested in what lay hidden beneath Gillian's towel. And if Conner was right about her past abuse, it could very well be a while before he'd have a chance to explore her body.

Remembering Conner's words, Max looked at her exposed flesh with new eyes. He picked up every discoloration and marking which marred her beautiful complexion. Conner had been right. Someone had harmed Gillian, grabbing, pulling, and possibly even hitting her hard enough to leave bruises. Some looked weeks old while the one on her neck looked fresh and new.

He wasn't sure how long he stood there and stared at her, but by the time he finally snapped out of it, her light blush had deepened to a bright red. Max stepped into the shower and dropped to his knees before her, placing his jars on the ground.

"Here, you hold this," Max handed her some bandages, "while I treat these sores."

He wrapped his palm around her calf and raised her foot, propping it on his thigh. She jerked her foot back as if scalded.

"I can take care of it. Just leave the stuff with me and I'll be fine."

"No, I'll put the salve on and bandage you up."

He was doubly careful when he picked her foot back up and replaced it on his thigh. She jerked it away again.

"Gilly, will you put your foot on my leg so I can take care of you already?"

She didn't seem to notice when he grabbed her leg again and began working on applying the salve.

"Gilly? Since when did I become Gilly?"

Raw sores and blisters covered the tops and sides of her foot, but the sole seemed to have fared well during her trek. With soft touches, he smoothed the sticky medicine on her various injuries before wrapping her foot in gauze. Removing her foot from his thigh and grabbing the other, he answered her.

"From the moment Conner told me your name was Gillian."

She snatched her foot away again. Damn, the spirits were testing him. He was going to have to develop the personality of a saint if he had any hope of getting through this. Every time he moved the towel rode higher on her thighs. Soon, he'd be staring at her sweet mound, and more than anything, he wanted a taste.

"You're not Conner!"

Sighing, he placed her foot back on his thigh. Of course she snatched it away again.

"Of course I'm not Conner, I'm Max. Do I look like Conner to you?" He held up his hand to stave off her reply. "Never mind, don't answer that. To you, I must look like him."

He picked up her foot. Before he even got it to his thigh she'd snatched it back again. This was really beginning to annoy him.

"You could have said something when you came in. I asked for Conner."

Sitting back, he let his eyes travel to hers. "Conner and Ronan are making our dinner and I'm the one in the family who knows first aid. I'm sorry I didn't say something right away, but I tend to forget not everyone can tell us apart." Running his hands through his hair, he dropped his eyes to his lap. His cock was getting very interested in his half-clothed mate, even if she was pissed. "If you want Conner to come in and bandage you up…?"

"No," she cut him off. "I was just surprised, that's all. You've…you've been nothing but kind to me. Please, I appreciate you taking care of me."

This time she placed her foot in his lap without his urging and when his eyes moved back to hers, she gifted him with the most amazing smile he'd ever seen. It was as if the spirits had gifted him with the sight of heaven in his home.

Max broke eye contact before he embarrassed himself, instead focusing his attention on the task of treating Gillian's foot. When that was done, he rolled to his feet, but bent down to look her in the eyes.

"I've taken care of your feet, how about I take care of your neck as well?."

The blood drained from her face, leaving it deathly pale and her eyes dropped to her twined fidgeting fingers.

"I'm fine," she whispered in a tiny voice, almost too low to hear.

"No, you're not, Gilly. You've got some nasty bruising. If I was a betting man, I'd think someone did this to you."

"No." Her eyes shot to his. "I…" She licked her lips and he could practically see the wheels spinning in her head as she sought a good lie.

"Let me guess, you had a run-in with a door?"

Gillian's eyes dropped to her folded hands. "Yes, that's right, a door."

Sure it was.

"A door that happened to have four fingers and an opposable thumb?" His hands covered hers, stopping her from rubbing and twisting them together while stealing her attention. "Gilly, you don't have to tell me who it was, just tell me if they're coming after you. My brothers and I want to help you, but we can't if we don't know some of what's going on."

Tears threatened to pour from her eyes and his heart broke for her. From what he could see of her body, it was apparent she was a strong woman who was willing to fight.

Sniffling, she shared her story with him.

"The door's name is Kyle. He's been following me for about a week and keeps finding me. This…" she gestured to her neck, "is from the last time he found me. I don't want to drag you three into this. I just need some time to rest and then I'll be on my way."

"Gilly, how are you going to get out of here without a car? Without warm clothes? You go out in the blizzard and you're as good as dead."

Wiping the tears away, she stared at him. "My car broke down at the beginning of your driveway. But I'd rather the elements take me to my death than him."

He believed it. Max felt the truth of her words through his soul and knew if push came to shove, Gillian would rather die in the cold than by Kyle's hand.

"Okay, Gilly. We'll take a look at your car tomorrow if the weather allows it. But you're staying with us until it's fixed. There's no way we'll allow you to go traipsing through the mountain side dressed in jeans and sneakers."

"But he'll find me. And he'll find you. I don't want that."

"And we'll protect you, Gilly." As if possessed, he cupped her cheek and his thumb brushed away her single escaped tear . "The Bearclaw brothers can take care of themselves and, if you'll let us, won't let anything happen to you either."

Straightening, he grabbed the robe Conner had hung on a nearby hook and held it open for her. "Now, if we're done arguing, let's go see what Ronan and Conner have made for us, shall we?"

Max turned his head as she stood, trying not to look at her nude body when she dropped the towel. He winced in empathy when she groaned—the salve had some anesthetic properties, but it couldn't take away all of her pain. When she slid her arms in, he released his hold and allowed her to wrap it around her body. After she tightened the tie and turned around, he scooped her into his arms, laughing at her high-pitched squeak.

"All set, beautiful?"

Gillian slid her arms around his neck and he nearly groaned at her touch. When she laid her head on his shoulder, her breath feathered across his skin and his cock took notice.

"All set."

Chapter Four

Gillian stretched her tired, aching muscles as she snuggled under the covers in the Bearclaws' guest bedroom. Over dinner she'd found out the room she guessed was the guest room wasn't the guest room at all. It was Ronan's.

That had been an embarrassing moment. Sitting around their kitchen table, scarfing down the dinner Conner and Ronan had made, she nearly choked on a big hunk of steak when they told her. Face burning, her eyes shot to Ronan's. How could a man surrounded by so much happiness have such a sparse, cold room? His unblinking gaze rested on hers, as if challenging her, until she dropped her eyes to her plate. His look spoke volumes; Ronan was a man who had lived through a tremendous pain which he still carried with him every day.

Their dinner continued, peppered with bursts of laughter as the three men told stories of their childhood. They'd told her all sorts of things about them under the guise of storytelling and she'd realized they were good men. Now she felt more comfortable around the three of them than she had when she'd first awoken. After the brief conversation in the bathroom with Max, no one brought up her bruises or why she wandered the miles down their road. They treated her like an old friend stopping over for dinner.

When Conner scooped her into his arms and carried her to the guest bedroom, Gillian didn't protest. She was starting to get used to being carried around by the brothers. Then again, Ronan still hadn't touched her and she wasn't sure if she wanted him to.

The cold look in his eyes frightened yet intrigued her. In one heartbeat she felt the need to comfort and kiss the hurt away and in the next, she wanted to cower behind Max and Conner. It was crazy. She shouldn't want to do anything with any of them. And yet she did.

Closing her eyes against the soft lamplight in the bedroom, she pictured the three of them in her mind. The natural honey tone of their skin pronounced their Native American heritage proudly. Their hair was cut short, but there was enough for a woman to wrap her fingers around. *Not that she wanted to, or anything.* And then there were their eyes. They were the color of the deep blue sea and Gillian half expected to see dolphins swimming in their depths.

Once she'd finally calmed down, dinner had been the perfect opportunity to stare at all three of them. True, they were triplets, but there were subtle differences between them. With the three of them surrounding her at the table, she could see it now. Max was quick to smile and crack a joke, never seeming to take anything seriously while they talked and threw insults at one another. Ronan's personality seemed to venture to the opposite side of the spectrum. Smiles came, but seldom and never quite reached his eyes. Conner appeared to be a balance between the two of them with easy smiles with and a hint of vulnerability which lingered beneath the surface. Their muscular bodies were the same, but inside they were all different.

Geez! *Their bodies!* Their muscles had muscles. Every inch she could see seemed chiseled and cut from stone. With broad shoulders tapering to trim waists, she wondered if they each sported a set of washboard abs beneath their shirts. Their thighs bulged and shifted with each step they took and she snuck more than one look at their backsides as they moved around the kitchen, preparing their meal. *Heaven.* Gillian was in hot man heaven and she didn't want to ever leave. Too bad she would…soon. Kyle didn't leave her any choice.

Rolling over, she stared at the wall. Sleep wasn't coming and her bladder was making itself known. Throwing the covers off, she hung her feet off the edge of the bed and stared at the floor. Walking would have to happen to get to the bathroom down the hall, but she wasn't looking forward to it. Damn, it was going to hurt, but what could she do about it—nothing. Easing off of the bed, her breath came in great puffs as she bit her tongue to keep from crying out. *Fuck! It hurt!*

Padding across the room, one aching step at a time, Gillian took a deep, calming breath when she reached the doorway. Even with the salve and bandages, the pressure of walking on her feet sent slices of pain up her legs. Fighting the urge to moan and groan with each step, she leaned against the closed bedroom door as she caught her breath. The seconds ticked by as she waited for the majority of the pain to subside. Gathering her resolve, she twisted the knob on the door and opened it to the pitch-black hallway.

The moment her foot stepped across the threshold, the door opposite hers burst open and Ronan stood before her. Gillian jumped in surprise, her muscles tensing as her heart beat like a hummingbird's wings in her chest and she let out a small squeak. Her hand flew to cover her mouth, preventing any further sound from escaping.

"What are you doing out of bed?"

Even when he whispered his voice was harsh. Narrowing her eyes at him, she answered his question. "I have to go to the bathroom. Does no one have to pee in the middle of the night in this house?"

Okay, maybe that was a little harsh and bitch-esque, but he deserved it. He'd growled and snapped at her from the moment he'd found her in their home and now he was growling at her because she had to pee.

He stepped closer to her, closing the distance between them. "Of course we go to the bathroom, but you shouldn't be walking."

"What do you expect me to do? Yell the house down and wait for one of you to carry me to the bathroom?"

"Yes," he snapped, biting the word out so quickly she barely saw his mouth move.

"Well, too bad. I appreciate you three taking care of me this evening, but I'm feeling much better and… Omph!"

He ruined her tirade. Just when she had gotten her rant going, he ended it by scooping her into his arms. What was with the Bearclaw brothers and carrying her around?

Wrapping her arms around Ronan's neck to steady herself, she twisted her fingers around the hair at the base of his skull and pulled.

"Ow!"

"Good. Put. Me. Down."

It took him several strides to reach the open bathroom door and she tugged and wiggled with each of his steps.

"Stop moving, dammit."

He moved through the doorway with her squirming body without hitting the doorjamb. Plopping her down on the toilet lid, he strode back to the door, flipping the lights on as he passed the switch. Grabbing the doorknob, he pulled it behind him, pausing long enough to issue a few orders.

"Sit there and pee. When you're done, *call me,* and I will come get you and take you back to bed."

Yanking the door closed with a soft click, Gillian stuck her tongue out at the man on the other side of the door. *Jerk.*

Taking care of business, Gillian made sure her makeshift pajamas were in place before calling for her erstwhile escort.

"Ronan!" she whispered as loud as she dared. The whole house didn't need to wake up because she had to use the bathroom.

He came into the room just as she was hobbling toward the sinks to wash her hands. Growling, he picked her up and plopped her onto the counter.

"What is with you and carrying me? I have two feet, ya know. It may hurt, but I am able to walk."

Ronan mumbled something in response while he turned the tap on and grabbed a washcloth from a nearby towel rung. She watched as he soaked the cloth and rubbed it with soap with quick, efficient movements. When he reached for her hands, she snatched them back.

"What was that? I didn't hear you." She tilted her head to the side and raised her brow.

As cliché as it sounded, if looks could kill, she'd be dead. Apparently one in the morning was not the time to tease Ronan. Not that any time seemed to be the right time. He reached for her hands and she allowed him to take hold of her wrist and she wiggled her fingers in his grasp, waving hello.

"Ronan…" She sung his name, prodding him.

Dropping the washcloth into the sink he braced his weight on the counter and stared at her, his sea blue eyes darkening to nearly black. "You deserve to be treated like fine china, Gillian. We like caring for you, which includes carrying you from place to place. Hell, when your feet are healed we'll probably still be carrying you around just to feel your skin against ours."

Oh. So not funny.

Thrusting her hands out, she stared at the wall over his shoulder, praying he couldn't see the hurt in her eyes. *We like caring for you? Feeling your skin against ours?* Yeah, right. And Gillian was the next president of the United States. As. If.

The brothers barely knew her. They'd been acquainted for a few hours and they liked taking care of her. They were definitely taking chivalry a little too far.

Ronan grasped her hands in his and wiped them down with the soaped washcloth, treating her as if she were a child who couldn't wash her own hands. It irked her. No, it pissed her off he treated her this way. She'd stood up to Kyle. She wasn't a victim any longer, but a survivor. She'd be damned if she tolerated being railroaded by anyone. When he rinsed her hands and dried them, she jumped down from the counter while he replaced the damp towel.

The moment her feet touched the floor pain shot through her legs and her knees buckled under the agony. Gillian crumpled to the floor in a moaning heap and gasped when one of her newest bruises collided with the tile floor. *FuckFuckFuck. Fuck!*

Ronan acted predictably, growling and pulling her trembling body into his arms. He sat down on a stool she hadn't noticed before and cradled her in his lap. Whispering words she couldn't understand into her hair. And then she felt it and froze—Ronan was pressing soft kisses along her temple as he whispered.

Gillian's pain washed away under his rain of kisses and sweet words. Even if she couldn't understand him, she understood what he was trying to do. Wiping her cheeks, she found them covered in moisture. She was crying and hadn't realized it.

"You okay, Gilly?"

She melted as his rumbling, sweet voice washed over her when he used the nickname Max had given her.

"I'm okay."

His callused hand cupped her cheek and tilted her head back until they were looking each other in the eye.

"Gilly…" He licked his lips and she mirrored his action. "You're special. More than you realize, you're special to me and my brothers." Ronan's thumb wiped away a new tear. "We want to take care of you because it's what you deserve. Let us pamper you, Gilly."

Ronan was offering everything she'd ever wanted from a man. Only he was offering three men to pamper her, not one.

"Okay, while I'm here, I'll try to relax. It's just new, Ronan. I've never had a man take care of me before…"

He gave her a rueful smile. "Yeah, Max told us about your door."

Shame replaced the feelings of warmth that had begun winding their way through her body. Max had told them. *They knew.* They all knew of her mistake.

"Hey. It's not your fault. He is an insecure dick with legs. Our mother taught us better. Yeah, the world has quite a few 'doors' wandering around who should be turned into kindling. But nothing's going to happen to you while you're here, okay?"

Nodding, she laid her head on his shoulder while his hand caressed her cheek.

"Thank you, Ronan, but I don't want to be a burden to you all and I don't want to bring Kyle to your door. It's not your fight. I'm a stranger to you…"

"Shhh…" His hand traveled from her cheek to stroke her neck, shoulder, and skim along her arm leaving goose bumps in its wake. A near stranger's touch shouldn't feel so good, so right.

Snuggling closer to Ronan, pressing more of her body to his chest, her hand traveled and came to rest at the juncture of his neck and shoulder. Closing her eyes, she relaxed into the embrace of a man for the first time in years.

"Gilly?"

"Hm?"

"Going to take you to bed now, okay?"

Sliding her hand to the back of his neck, she stroked his skin before burying her fingers in his hair. She loved doing that, sifting through the silken strands with her fingers made her feel closer to a man.

With half-closed eyes she raised her head and looked at Ronan, really looked at him. She couldn't believe she ever thought the Bearclaw brothers were identical. In her eyes, they were far from it.

Ronan licked his lips in a gesture she was beginning to recognize as a nervous habit. Seemed *she* made *him* nervous. *Good.*

Seconds ticked by and Ronan slowly closed the difference between them. She just wanted him to kiss her already! He was probably trying to give her time to protest, but she wasn't going to protest. She wanted his lips on hers. *Now.*

Then it happened. Ronan brushed his lips across hers, a tentative caress and gliding of his skin against her lips and she felt her nerve endings come alive. His tongue emerged and licked the seam of her lips. He didn't have to ask twice, she opened for him, offering her mouth eagerly.

At her acquiescence, his tongue bombarded her mouth, swirling and dueling with her own until she surrendered completely. Ronan's tongue explored every corner of her mouth, sliding and caressing every surface before sucking her tongue and releasing her briefly to nip her lower lip. The sensual sting shot through her body and straight to her core.

The kiss didn't end there. His tongue returned, plunging into her very depths, scorching her soul with his kiss. Their tongues mimicked the dance they both ached for, but before it could go any further, Gillian pulled away.

It was moving too far, too fast. They'd just met and she was making out with him in the middle of the night, in the bathroom of all places. Every cell in her body screamed and begged her to return to his kiss, but her brain told her to quit acting easy.

They were both breathing hard, the sounds echoing in the small room and she couldn't look at him. If she did, she'd start kissing him again.

Staring at his chest, she wouldn't look at his face out of fear of what she'd see there, she spoke, barely a whisper.

"You said something about bed?"

Oh! That was so freaking dumb! Now he'll think I want him to join me! Don't I want him to join me? No. No, I don't. At least not yet.

"Right." He took a deep breath, forcing his chest to press against hers. "Bed."

"Bed alone."

"Alone. Right."

In one smooth move he was standing with Gillian in his arms and striding toward the open bathroom door. In seconds she was back in the guest room and he sat her on the bed.

Ronan held the covers up, probably so she could crawl beneath them, but she wasn't ready to lie down. Not yet.

"It's okay, I've got to get comfortable and then I'll crawl in."

She tried to give him a "get the hell out of here" smile, but it didn't work. Or, he just refused to catch the hint.

"Gilly, didn't I just tell you I want to take care of you? That includes tucking you in, unless the kiss changed that and you just want me to get the hell out of here."

Okay, he understood the look, but not the reason. Great.

"Ronan, I'm going to spell it out for you and embarrass the hell out of myself at the same time. The kiss was amazing. Freaked me the hell out, but amazing nonetheless. I want you to leave because I plan on taking these pajama bottoms off and if you'll recall, my laundry wasn't done when you guys gave me clothes to sleep in."

It finally got through to him.

"Oh. Oh!" He gave her a wicked smile, one that reached his eyes and she didn't think she'd ever seen a more beautiful sight. "You sure you don't want my help?"

Laughing at him as he wiggled his eyebrows, she shook her head.

"Thank you for the offer, but no."

"Fine." He stuck out his lower lip, but leaned forward for a quick kiss before turning and heading for the door. "Night, Gilly."

"Night, Ronan."

Chapter Five

Ronan pulled the door closed as he stepped over the threshold of Gillian's room and into the hallway. Leaning against the closed door, he willed his heart to slow as he listened to the sounds emanating from behind the door.

The rustle of the bed sheets reached him a moment before a soft gasp tore through his heart. He could imagine her standing on shaky legs and aching feet as she wiggled out of her pajama bottoms. A creak of wood met his ears and he knew she'd crawled back into bed. The sheets rustled again, probably as she pulled them across her body, now half-clothed, and the distinct click of the lamp being turned off echoed through the room.

Standing outside her door and listening to her breathe would surely drive him crazy. Pushing away from the door, he took a few steps and was embraced by the familiar surroundings of his own room. But something was different. The scent of vanilla, lavender, and mint that seemed to surround Gillian remained. He'd never get any sleep.

Accepting his fate, Ronan flopped onto his bed, throwing on arm over his eyes. It was going to be a long night indeed. Her fragrance wrapped around his body, skimming and flowing through his pores where he lay. His cock, half hard from Gillian's kiss, slowly filled with blood until it strained against his boxers. Sitting up, Ronan peeled off his t-shirt before lying down again. Damn, it was hot in his room.

Closing his eyes, he imagined Gillian lying in bed with him. Not the Gillian across the hall, but a Gillian who had a soul filled with trust. A woman whose skin wasn't marred with bruises caused by a man and fear didn't lurk in her eyes. His mate was a beautiful woman, but she'd be breathtaking when she could be in a room with all three of them and not spend every moment searching for an escape route. The "door", Kyle, would be in a world of hurt if he ever came to their home.

The open, trusting Gillian in his imagination would snuggle against his body, lining up every one of her curves against him. From the brief glimpses he'd had of her body and the few times he held her, Ronan knew her body was plump and curvaceous, just the way the Bearclaw men liked their women. With her pressed against him, one hand would bury in her golden, bouncing curls while the other would stroke her body from shoulder to hip, savoring the silken smoothness beneath his work roughened hands.

She'd sigh against his chest, enjoying the soft touches. Ronan would be gentle, oh so gentle, with his Gilly. She deserved to be caressed and that's what she'd get. Her hands would sift through the hair on his chest and find his nipple, rubbing, stroking, and pinching the tiny nubbin.

Ronan mimicked the actions of his imaginary Gillian, touching his body as he imagined she would. His fingers found their mark and he pinched, shivering as the sensation peaked and slithered away. His hand released the tiny protrusion of flesh, hardened from his touch, and snaked his hand south. With light touches, he imagined Gillian tempting and teasing him by stroking his abdomen, to his hip, and then thighs before repeating the caress. He did the same, driving his need higher.

Refusing to break free of his fantasy, Ronan continued. Stroking, touching, feeling, his muscles tensed beneath his fingers before relaxing as his hand inched closer to its goal. So much closer. After a few more teasing touches, his fingertips sifted through the cropped curls surrounding his erection and stroked the base of his shaft.

Hard as a rock, his thumb and forefinger encircled his hardness and squeezed, relishing in the first touch of his sensitive skin. Dragging his hand up his erection, his fingers picked up the silken drop of pre-come and rubbed it on the tip. Gasping at the sensation, he encircled his shaft once again and using his pre-come as a lubricant, began stroking his cock again. He imagined it was Gillian's hand loving his body, and the speed of stroke increased. Up, down, up, squeeze. Over and over he moved his hand on his body. Gilly would be so sweet, so perfect at loving him.

Hips moving in conjunction with his hand, he continued the gentle tugging and stroking of his erection while his other hand moved to cup his balls. Imagining it was Gillian's mouth tonguing him, he rolled the sensitive sack in his hand, alternating between tugging and squeezing. The combination of the fantasy and self-loving was pulling him closer to the edge. Any moment now he'd come with thoughts of Gillian dominating his mind.

At one point, Ronan brought his feet closer to his body, knees bent. He began thrusting into his hand, pretending it was Gillian's plump mouth encircling his cock, sucking him dry. Her tongue would swirl and stroke the large vein of his shaft. Flicking the spot just below his cock's crown would drive him mad with want.

Ronan's orgasm built, shimmering beneath his skin as it ran along his nerves and centered in his lower back. It pushed and rushed against the confines of his body, begging to be released. He increased his movements. Tightening his hand on his shaft, he thrust harder, pulled and tugged on his balls, squeezing them almost to the point of pain. Sweat poured from his brow, his body cried for release.

His movements continued. On and on they went as he reached for his release. His mind dove back into his fantasy of Gillian giving him pleasure. She'd suck and moan around his shaft, tempting and cajoling his come from its haven. *Spirits,* how he wanted to give it to her.

Closing his eyes, he imagined looking down at Gillian, her mouth stretched around his erection, love shining from her eyes as she sucked him and then he jumped. His body arched, muscles tensing as his seed burst from the tip of his cock. The tension that had built in his balls released in a rush. It felt as if his insides were bursting through his cock, tensing, releasing in time with his heartbeat.

Seconds later, his back still arched, cock still half-hard, he eased his body back to the bed. His breath still came in harsh pants as his mind returned to the present. His imaginary Gillian, the woman that gave so willingly with trust shining from her eyes, whispered out of his mind, and he felt an ache in his heart at the loss. But she would return to him again. He only hoped that next time she wouldn't be imaginary. She would be the woman across the hall, loving his body like no other woman could or ever would.

Grabbing his discarded t-shirt, Ronan wiped the cooling come off of his hand and abdomen. Throwing it on the ground next to the bed, he rolled over, dragging the sheets with him and drifted off to sleep.

* * *

Raised, angry voices pulled Gillian from her sweet slumber. Opening her eyes, she was assaulted by the bright sunlight streaming through the window.

Damn, it must be late.

Raising her arms above her head, she stretched and groaned as her muscles, joints and bruises ached in protest. Just about every part of her body hurt. But, at least they weren't new hurts, right? Sure, she'd gone to bed sore and tired, but not with any new cuts or bruises of someone else's making.

The voices of the Bearclaw brothers drew her attention.

"No, you're not." *Ronan.*

"Yes, I am." *Conner, maybe?*

"Guys, now, calm down." *Definitely Max.*

But what were they arguing about?

"You're not going in there until she's up and dressed."

"What makes you think she's not? Did you take advantage of her last night? You did, didn't you?"

But Ronan hadn't. He'd been surprisingly sweet and gentle and gave her a kiss that curled her toes. He'd even left when she asked him to without putting up a fight or forcing himself on her. She'd seen and felt the erection he was sporting, but he didn't pressure her to do anything about it. Who was Conner to accuse him of something like that?

"Conner, Ronan hasn't done anything beyond asking you to give Gilly her privacy, right, Ronan? You're not insinuating…?"

"No, don't stick-up for me, Max, Conner thinks I'm the type of man to take advantage, maybe I did."

He did not!

She snatched up her discarded pajama bottoms from the ground and tugged them on, tightening them as much as she could, and prayed they stayed on her hips. They were at least eight inches too long, but there wasn't anything she could do about it now. Shuffling across the room, she reached the door just as the distinct sound of flesh hitting flesh reached her ears.

Her heart stopped for a moment, pausing between beats as her mind filtered the knowledge that three very large men, two of whom were hitting each other, stood on the other side of the wooden door. Should she open it and clear the air, or lock it tight against their intrusion and escape through the window?

Blood thundered through her body and all she could hear now was the rapid beating of her heart as her body infused with adrenaline. Her hand gripped the knob, knuckles whitening from the pressure of her hold. Her breath came fast and hard, as her thoughts warred with her body. The men had shown her nothing but kindness, yet they were fighting, getting physical over entering her room. No! Her mind screamed while the other half yelled at her to open the door, end the torment.

She wanted to run in two directions at once. *To the window, or through the door?* Frozen, she clutched the knob as the voices continued, but she couldn't hear any evidence of a continued fight.

"Feel better now?" *Ronan.*

He was okay. Her grip remained on the knob, even if she felt like sagging against the door in relief.

"Asshole."

"That I am."

"Move, Max."

Feet moved on the other side of the door, their shadows peeking beneath the wood. Her heart had begun to slow at hearing the low growl of Ronan's voice, but it was quickly picking up speed once again. Now was the time to flick the lock. *Now!*

But she couldn't. The sweet way Conner took care of her when she first arrived, the tender touches Max gave her as he cared for her cuts and the softest most touching kiss she'd ever received from Ronan made her hand freeze on the knob. They'd proven their tenderness and caring toward her, she couldn't let Conner attack Ronan. Couldn't.

"Conner, I don't think now's the time…"

"You're not going in there, Conner."

"Watch me, Ronan."

"Guys, this is becoming a bit like a pissing match only you're pissing gas and she's the match. Do you really want to go in there as pissed off as you are?"

Silence reigned then the sound of bare feet padding down the hall met her ears. They'd left. Maybe she could sneak into the living room and grab her shoes and then…well, she didn't know what. She just knew their fighting freaked her the fuck out.

Turning the knob, she opened the door on its silent hinges and was met with what she could only guess was Max's back. Fuck!

He must have heard her gasp, or breathe, or something because he whirled around. His furrowed brow and look of worry was quickly replaced with an easy smile—so much like Ronan's, but different.

"Mornin', beautiful."

He greeted her as if he hadn't just broken up a fight between his brothers. Like everything was as it should be in the world.

"Max?"

"Yep, you're getting better at telling us apart."

Grunts and a thump against the house could be felt through the floor. Max coughed, pounding his chest and stamping his foot. Was she supposed to believe that the sound had come from him? Did she look like an idiot?

"Where are Ronan and Conner?"

The fear still waged a war against her compassion, but she didn't like the idea of the two men fighting. The fact that the fight had been taken outside, she presumed to keep her from hearing, made her feel a little better, but she couldn't let them beat the crap out of each other.

"Uh. Around."

His body blocked the entire doorway, his shoulders nearly touching the sides of the doorjamb. She scooted as quickly as her feet would allow to the left, but he was too quick for her. She stepped back to look him in the eye.

"Around?"

"Uh huh."

She feigned right and moved her body left, but he blocked her again. Stepping back, she planted her hands on her hips and glared at Max.

"Why are you keeping me locked in here, Max?"

"Uh. What makes you think I am?"

"Max?" She growled his name, low and as menacing as she could make it. "Do I look like an idiot to you?" She held up her hand. Max had proved to be the laid-back jokester of the family and she'd just walked him into the perfect set-up. "Wait, don't answer that. Just tell me why I can't go outside where it's obvious Conner and Ronan are doing their best to kill each other."

Leaning against the doorjamb, Max looked defeated, his smile turning into a grimace as the seconds ticked by and grunts of pain could be heard from outside.

"They didn't want to scare you. They're working out their differences the only way they know how and well, they don't want you thinking of them as another 'door', beautiful. We all like you, *a lot,* and want you to feel safe and happy here. They didn't think fighting in the hallway outside your bedroom would make you feel safe or happy."

Fuck if that wasn't what she thought when she heard the first punch connect. Now, knowing that this just was the way they were, she wanted it to stop.

"I'm going out there, Max, and you can't stop me."

"Gillian, I really think it'd be best if we stayed inside until they're done."

"No." She'd made up her mind. Couldn't he see that?

Running his hands through his hair, she could practically see the wheels spinning as he tried to think of a different stalling tactic. But, he ended up repeating a phrase that was familiar and oddly comforting.

"I'm carrying you."

Victory!

Of course, her victory was short lived. When he bent to pick her up, she expected to be cradled in his arms like all three of the men had done before. Instead, he threw her over his shoulder like a sack of potatoes, ass straight up in the air.

"Max! Put me down!"

Chuckling as he strode down the hallway, his hand moved up and down the backs of her thighs and she couldn't stop the shiver that raced through her. What kind of slut was she to get aroused by the brother of the man she'd kissed the night before?

When he reached the door, he flung it open and stepped into the bright, frigid morning air.

Fuck, it's cold!

Smacking his lower back didn't have any effect on the man. That had been proven by every hit she'd rained on him as he walked through the house. Aiming lower, she smacked his ass, which earned her a swat in return.

"Hey!"

"Hey yourself!" He laughed, deep and hard. She felt it through her entire body.

Max strode around the wrap-around porch until they were within earshot of Conner and Ronan fighting. Gillian could hear their pants, grunts and moans as they fought. Hitting Max's back, she yelled at him.

"Put me down or turn me around, I want to see!"

Spinning, she squeaked when she felt like he'd drop her, but his hold was steady. Conner and Ronan were locked together, arms twisting, pulling, squeezing and fighting for dominance as they rolled around in the snow, ice, and mud. They weren't punching each other so much as they were wrestling. This wasn't about one beating the other unconscious, but resembled two kids fighting in the schoolyard.

The tension she hadn't known was with her released, but it was quickly replaced with agitation. Stupid men! Worrying her, making her fret and contemplate running because they wanted to wrestle like animals. Max had been right. It was a great big pissing contest.

She poked Max in the side as she issued her orders.

"Take two steps back and move left." She waited while he moved as she directed. "No, no, your other left. Perfect."

Her goal was within arm's reach. Gillian scooped a handful of snow off the railing and formed it into a small ball, compacting the snow as tightly as she could. It needed to both sting and stun the men she had her sights on.

Thanking her brother for being into baseball and needing someone to throw with, she let the first ball fly. It hit Ronan in the shoulder, drawing his attention away from Conner, which resulted in him being laid out by his brother. She heard Ronan yelling, but was focused on gathering another clump of snow and forming the perfect ball to really pay attention. Conner distracted him again, so she supposed it didn't matter. Taking aim, she let her second snowball fly and got Conner in the back of the head. Max had remained perfectly still through her two lobs, but was now on the move and striding across the porch.

"Max! What are you doing, I'm not done!"

"But they are, Gilly, and they're ready to turn their attentions to us."

Glancing back at Conner and Ronan, she realized that Max was right. They had both jumped up and were stomping toward the porch. Smacking Max on the ass, she urged him to move.

"Run, Max, they're coming!" Giggles fought with the twinge of fear over what would happen when the two hulking men caught them.

Max made it through the front door before his brothers caught them and plopped her down on the couch in the living room and stood between her and his brothers.

"Move it, Max," Conner and Ronan barked.

"Okay." He held his hands up and moved out of their way.

So much for my valiant protector.

"Uh, guys. It was a joke. I got mad at you for fighting and…"

They were on her in a second. Tickling every inch of her body they could get their hands on. Growling when they got a good spot and her laughter filled the room, smearing mud and melted snow all over her. By the time she cried "uncle", she was soaked and covered in mud from head to toe, as was the couch and a good part of the floor.

Gasping for air, she sat on the couch between the two men. Remembering why she'd gone outside with Max in the first place, she smacked both of their thighs.

"You idiots! You scared me half to death! One minute I thought you were going to break down the door and the next I thought you were going to kill each other. Don't you ever do that again—at least, not during my visit."

The three brothers shared a look before Ronan spoke. "Sorry, Gillian. We've been together, just the three of us, for a long time and tend to settle disagreements with fists." She'd turned her attention to him the moment he began speaking and she leaned into his touch when he cupped her cheek. It seemed so natural and reminded her of the kiss they'd shared the night before. She didn't jump or pull back when his lips brushed hers.

A warm hand encircled her wrist and out of the corner of her eye, she could see Max crouched before her. He pressed a tender kiss to the palm of her right hand and when another set of lips kissed the palm of her left…it felt right.

Chapter Six

Two hours, four showers, two eggs, bacon, toast, and a coffee later, Gillian didn't know what to do with herself. She watched as Conner and Ronan bumped down the driveway and out of sight in their four-wheel drive pick-up truck, complete with towing wench. They'd promised that their trip out would result in warm clothes for her and the return of her car, one way or another.

She prayed that the "one way" they hinted at was not that her car would be towed behind their truck. Because that would mean that the hunk of metal wouldn't start. It was just something she wasn't ready to consider yet. Being in their cabin, surrounded by their presence was all right short-term.

When their lips touched her body, all at the same time, she'd felt a zing of awareness shoot through her. It skittered along her nerves, just beneath the skin and materialized as a foreign awareness in her mind. Almost as if she could… *No. That wasn't possible.*

The novelty of having three identical men giving her three nearly identical looks and kisses was toying with her mind. Better to nip those thoughts in the bud now. No sense in imagining or interpreting their attentions for anything other than simple old-world chivalry. Nothing more.

Okay, maybe Ronan's kiss was more. The quiet, brooding type didn't usually catch her attention, but maybe things were changing. For the better, she hoped. With Ronan's apparent claim by capturing her lips when he apologized, Gillian wondered how he'd react to the knowledge that his brothers had kissed her palms. Would he be jealous? Would Ronan hand out a few bruises to Conner and Max as soon as they were alone? She hoped not. More than anything, she didn't want violence or dissention to arise from her attraction to Ronan.

Who was she kidding, she was attracted to all of them. They should bring a tattoo artist back with them and have "Hopeless Slut" tattooed to her forehead. At least then people would know what type of person they were talking to. The type that would wander into a home, fall asleep in someone's bed, wake to three gorgeous men staring at her, and after a series of events that made her head spin just thinking about, fantasize about all three of them—separately, and together. S. L. U. T.

"Whatcha thinking about over there? So serious."

Heat suffused her face, but she ignored it.

"Nothing," she lied.

"Uh huh."

Flopping onto the center of the couch right next to her, he pulled her feet into his lap before she could utter a protest. Not that she would protest…well, maybe a token protest, but she would've given in, which made the attempt at a protest pointless. So she didn't.

Max clicked the TV on, but lowered the volume before tossing the remote onto the coffee table. He must have seen her confused look because he answered her unvoiced question.

"Background noise. Can't stand a quiet house."

"Oh."

"So, Miss Gillian No-last-name, tell me about yourself."

"Maybe I'm an axe-murderer out to get you."

She'd play coy and joke her way through this. Thinking and speaking of the truth just hurt.

Max's hand encircled her wrist and slid up her arm, past her elbow to her bicep. He squeezed for a fraction of a second before opening his hand and nudging the side of her breast and then squeezing again. She gasped and jerked against his hold, but didn't push him away.

The surreptitious touch felt too good, sending tingles of arousal through her body. Gillian's nipples tightened in response, pushing against the cotton t-shirt she'd borrowed from Conner.

"No offense, Gilly, but you haven't got the muscles for it." He opened and closed his hand again, fingers brushing the sensitive skin through cloth before sliding his hand back to her wrist, his eyes locked on her the whole time. "How about your last name?"

Did he see the truth in her eyes? That she was as aroused by his touch as she was by Ronan's kisses.

"Locke." Had her voice dropped a few decibels?

"Miss Gillian Locke. Nice to meet you."

Max flashed a smile, but the teasing glint in his eyes had yet to leave. He was up to something.

His hand left her wrist and settled on the top of her thigh while the other stroked the calf on her other leg. She was wearing yet another pair of pajama bottoms donated by one of the brothers, so she was clothed, but for some reason she felt nearly naked under his gaze.

He traced tiny circles with his fingertips on top of the cloth, sometimes tracing the printed pattern for a while before returning to the miniscule circles. Was it getting hot in the cabin? Maybe they should put out the fire. Her eyes darted to the fireplace and noticed it was dark. *Damn, no fire.* Max's hand burrowed through the extra inches of fabric at the hem of the pants and felt their way up her pant leg.

The sensations of his skin on hers brought those feeling she'd been trying to ignore back. It was almost as if she could feel him feeling her. But that didn't make sense.

Swallowing hard, she forced words past her lips, words she didn't really mean, but thought she should voice.

"What are you doing? You shouldn't…"

"Shouldn't what? Shouldn't do this?" His hand beneath her pants rose higher, stroking every inch of skin he could. "Or this?" Max spread the fingers of the hand on her thigh, his thumb coming dangerously close to where she ached to be touched the most.

All she could do was moan.

S. L. U. T.

"Max, you don't understand. I don't want to get between you three and last night…"

"You kissed my brother."

She shot straight up.

"Exactly. Which is why your hands should stop…you *know*."

"Making you feel good? I can see your pulse in your neck, hear your breathing—you're enjoying this a little bit, Gilly. Don't deny it."

Oh, she wouldn't deny it, but she couldn't let him continue. She didn't owe Ronan anything, but making out with his brother didn't exactly feel right.

"I'm not going to deny it, but Max…"

"We share a special bond, Gillian. To find a woman we are all attracted to has been a lifelong dream of ours. Ronan won't be jealous or angry if I make you feel good." His hand on her thigh dipped lower, closer to her heat and he tightened his grip. One inch higher and he'd… "Let me make you feel good, Gillian."

She didn't say no, but she didn't say yes either. She whimpered. An honest-to-God whimper formed in her throat and emanated from behind her closed lips.

Max must have taken the noise for a yes. His body shifted and moved as he repositioned her legs to his choosing. Now she lay back on the couch, her legs on either side of his hips as he sat himself between them. A hungry, feral look passed over his face before he smiled. Her heart sped up, but quickly calmed when she saw his smile, his laid-back look instantly putting her at ease. Of course, that quickly ended when he ripped the crotch of her pajama bottoms right out, exposing the juncture of her thighs to the cool cabin air.

"Max!"

"Okay. Okay. Sorry. Just a little impatient." His hands grasped her upper thighs, thumbs rubbing along the skin where her leg and pelvis met. That sensitive area that only seemed to come alive under a man's touch tingled with every swipe of his thumb. "Better?"

What? Did he say something? Gillian wasn't sure. She was too busy enjoying what Max was doing with his hands. No man had ever touched her so intimately without rushing and with only regard to her enjoyment. This was…nice.

"Gillian?"

"Hmm?"

Her eyes drifted close as his hands stroked her body. She felt him shift and move, but the gentle assault of his fingers continued so she didn't bother opening her eyes. It felt so damn good. Her clit tingled and ached as it filled with blood. Her core clenched as his fingers shifted to her nether lips, and along the outer edge of her slit.

Gillian widened her legs, dropping one foot to the floor, she pressed her other knee into the cushions lining the back of the couch. Max's chuckle reached her ears as his breath feathered across her skin. Eyes flying open, she looked down her body into Max's. Her body tensed and she moved to close her thighs, but he wouldn't let her.

"Max?"

"So beautiful, Gillian. Especially here."

Beautiful was not what any man had called *that* area, ever. Odorous, maybe. *Oral sex on her?* Disgusting, from what Kyle said. What was he doing down there? His fingers worked just fine, thanks. He could sit up and pleasure her just as well.

"Max…"

"Please, Gillian. Just let me…"

She watched in open-mouthed awe as he lowered his lips to her pussy and licked a path from her ass to the top of her slit. His tongue skimmed her skin, not penetrating or separating the aching lips, but teasing them. Max's tongue disappeared into his mouth as he smiled.

"Delicious."

Delicious? No, she was *not* delicious.

Max leaned forward again and she held her breath, waiting for the feeling of his tongue on her again. This time, he pressed his face to her body, and inhaled. The sound echoed in the room.

"Heavenly. You smell like heaven."

Gillian was about to argue, but his tongue distracted her. Just when she opened her mouth to contradict him, he opened his and licked the top of her slit. Sifting through her curls, his tongue found her sensitive inner flesh and stroked it. She bit her lip to keep from crying out.

His fingers played again, stroking her outer lips before pulling them apart. He was looking at her, there. But when his tongue swiped her inner lips from core to clit, she didn't care. She only cared about the sensations he was causing in her body.

Arousal tingled and traveled through her body and her breasts felt fuller, heavier as her nipples tightened. God, how they needed to be pinched and pulled. The feelings didn't stop there though. They traveled, skittering along her nerves, making her feel as if her entire body was being touched and stroked.

Max's tongue continued its exploration of her heat, licking and sucking from clit to core and back again. He paused occasionally to thrust his tongue into her opening, flicking her inner walls and running his tongue around the rim. Damn, she needed something in there! She'd never craved something as much as she was craving a cock, a finger, something!

As if reading her mind, one of Max's hands abandoned its post of holding her open to him to thrust into her heat. Arching her back, she cried out, thankful for the large fingers filling her.

"That's it, Gilly. Damn, so sweet." His tongue swirled around her clit, causing her to moan and grind against his mouth.

"So." *Lick*.

"Fucking." *Flick*.

"Sweet." *Suck*.

It was the sucking that did it. She lost control. Her hands flew to tangle in his hair, pressing his head tighter against her pussy as she shifted and moved against him. His fingers, *damn*, his fingers did something magical within her body. They thrust and shifted in time with her movements until they pressed against her body in a way she'd never experienced.

Gillian's body clenched and tightened as she focused on the sensations Max was coaxing from her body. The muscles lining her inner core clenched and tightened around his fingers of their own volition. She'd lost the ability to restrain her body's response to him. His mouth latched onto her aching, pulsing clit and he sucked and flicked in time with his hand as he pushed her closer to completion. And she wanted it, wanted it so badly she could almost taste it.

His fingers worked her slick passage, thrusting, moving and sliding against that one special motion that made her body writhe in pleasure. The orgasm she'd been coaching and begging her body for burst forth in a tidal wave of sensation washing over her from head to toe, only to recede and rush forth again and again. Like a tightly strung string on a bow, she snapped, her back arching, as she pressed against his mouth and fingers as she screamed his name.

"Max!"

His mouth never stopped, his fingers continued. He kept time with her breathing, slowing as she did, allowing her to float languidly down from her orgasm high and back to earth, to his arms. He pressed soft kisses to her thighs, her mound, as she came back to herself. Relaxing into the cushions with a sigh, she whimpered when he withdrew his hand and watched in awe as he licked his fingers clean.

"Delicious. Thank you, Gilly."

"Thank me?"

Max rose up on all fours and crawled over her, pressing his considerable bulge to the juncture of her thighs. She could feel his hardness through his jeans and she felt needy, wanting.

He pressed his lips to her neck, inhaling as he rained kisses beneath her ear and along her jaw.

"Yes. Thank you for trusting me and sharing that bit of yourself with me."

He pulled back, brushing a kiss across her lips, her tongue snaked out, hoping for a kiss, but instead she was met with a hint of her own musk. Her arousal grew anew. Never had she done anything so risqué before. But before she had a chance to search out more of her own flavor on his lips, he lifted his body off of hers and stood next to the couch.

"Come on, Gilly. Conner and Ronan are almost home, let's get you changed."

His wicked smile was back and he winked at her before hoisting her body off the couch. Good thing he was doing the walking, she didn't think she'd be able to if she tried.

Chapter Seven

The scent hit him the moment he stepped from the truck. He didn't wait for Ronan to exit Gilly's car, which he'd towed behind the truck. Instead, he strode for the front door, ice and mud shifting beneath his feet as he made a beeline for the cabin.

The scent—God damn—the smell permeated the air surrounding the cabin, sifting through his clothes to seep into his skin. The scent of Gillian's arousal, like sweet, musky honey, wove through the planks and snuck through the cracks in the door to reach him.

He'd kill Max. The ass had fucked Gillian while they were out seeing to her car and personal needs. The moment they'd driven off the property he'd weaseled his way into her pants and claimed her. *Fucker!* They'd agreed, all of them, that the first time anyone made love to their Gillian they'd all be involved by either watching or participating. All of them, or none of them. Their lives would be shared from the first moment, and Max had ruined everything.

Conner threw the front door open, banging it against the wall with a thud.

"Max!" He didn't bother with removing his mud-caked shoes. Ronan would have to get over it.

"Max!" He tried to hold his breath and resist the effects of Gillian's scent on his beast. His cock hardened as he passed the living room, the scent seemed concentrated there. He veered to the right as he searched for his soon-to-be-dead brother, and found him exiting the kitchen, a dishtowel in his hands.

"What?"

Conner pulled his fist back and let it fly at Max's face. Unfortunately, Max ducked, causing Conner to swing at air and connect with the wood plank wall. Growling, he followed Max as his brother dashed around the kitchen table, placing it between them.

"What the fuck, Conner?"

"You're asking me that question? You ass. You fucked her. You fucked her the minute we were gone…!"

Ronan raced into the kitchen, sliding across the polished wood floor, the melting snow making the polished flooring slick. He came to a halt near the center of the table.

"I didn't!" Max threw his hands up. "I swear!"

"What the fuck do I smell then, asshole?"

Max had a satisfied, pussy-eating grin on his face and Conner wanted to shred the table to get to him and tear his brother apart.

"Now, Conner, hear him out." *Ronan, the voice of fucking reason.*

How could he want to hear Max out with the scent of Gillian's arousal and release infused in the very air they breathed? The heavy musk seeped into his pores and beckoned his beast, begging it to claim her. *Reason? Hear him out?* Maybe after he'd ripped Max to pieces first—teeny, tiny, itsy bitsy pieces.

"You smell a satisfied woman, but I swear we didn't have sex, Conner. I couldn't, I'd never…"

"You swear?" He growled, shoving the table into Max's groin. If he had fucked Gillian, he'd still be tender and if he hadn't, he'd still be hard. Conner got satisfaction out of hearing Max's grunt.

Max clutched his groin, a grimace of pain on his face. He croaked out a response. "I swear. I just pleasured her, Conner. I'd never do anything else without you two there."

Conner ran a hand through his hair, taking a deep breath. Bad idea, Gillian's scent still hung heavily in the air. He needed to get out of the cabin, away from the smell of her arousal and away from his brother's satisfied smirk. He may not have claimed their mate, but he sure as hell did something to her.

The need to mate or fight rode Conner hard as he stood, staring his brother Max down, but Ronan's words brought him back out of his anger filled haze.

"Do you really want to do this again? Have another fight with Gillian in the house? You saw how she reacted this morning." Damn Ronan for being sensible. He really wanted to tear a piece out of Max's hide. Hell, both of his brothers' hides. They'd gotten to touch her, spend time with her alone and relate to her in ways he had yet to. He wanted his time.

"You're right." Conner backed away from the table, shuffling until his back connected with the wall. He leaned his weight against it, taming his beast and calming his heart. He'd come too close to harming his brother—over a woman.

Once he'd calmed considerably, he raised his head, eyes meeting first Ronan's and then Max's.

"I'm sorry, Max. I just smelled… And I'm jealous as hell and my beast…"

"No sorry needed, Conner. Though, you may have put my equipment out of commission for a while." *Max, ever the joker.*

"Good. More for me later."

"Not if we tear each other apart first."

Ronan was right. Their father had warned them about this. The time between finding their center and claiming her could either bring brothers together, or tear them apart.

"That's not going to happen, Ronan. We won't let it happen."

"It nearly happened to Dad."

Conner dropped his head back, thumping it against the wood.

Max spoke up. "Just because our parents nearly killed one another, doesn't mean we will. We've agreed we won't make love to her without the other's presence, right?"

"Yeah," he grumbled. Conner wanted nothing more than to sink into her sweet depths, but he wouldn't. Not without Max and Ronan by his side.

"So, we won't. If, however, you can stimulate her and get her used to our touch, maybe making love with the three of us, opening her arms to us, won't be so difficult for her. She wasn't raised like us, guys. We need to remember, in her world, three men and one woman are the formula for bad orgy porn." Max, ever the master of the spoken language.

Connor pushed away from the wall, yet stared at his feet, trying to figure out where he could go to get away for a while. He needed to get out of the house, away from his brothers, and the temptation of Gillian.

"Fine." He knew just the place. He could prepare them for the cold winter's night and work off some of his energy at the same time. "I'm heading out for a while. Be back in a bit."

Turning toward the back door, he stomped through the house, leaving a trail of mud in his wake. Well, at least he knew what Ronan would be doing while he was gone.

* * *

Gillian pressed her ear to the door, trying to hear the conversation in the kitchen, but couldn't. She'd heard Conner yelling at Max, but their voices quickly dropped too low for her to make out. When she heard the stomping of boots and back door slam, she figured it was safe to come out. Somehow, she seemed to be the center of arguments between the three men, which could only mean one thing. It was time for her to go.

Hopefully, they'd fixed her car. If not, she'd be trekking through the snow on foot. She wasn't looking forward to it, but she couldn't come between the three brothers. And if she had to be honest with herself, their tendency toward violence frightened her.

She opened the door, then leaving the bathroom behind, she padded to the kitchen to find Ronan and Max sitting at the kitchen table. Both men wore grim expressions. *Yep, time to go.* Gillian wrapped her arms around her waist and cleared her throat to make her presence known.

"Hey Gilly." Max held an arm out to her. She wanted to run into his arms, let him tell her it wasn't her fault, she didn't have to leave. She ached to have someone to fall into, instead, she remained rooted to the spot.

"Gillian?" Ronan stared at her, eyes focused as if he tried to read her mind. She dropped her eyes to the floor.

"I'm, uh, leaving." She heard a startled "what" from Max, but Ronan must have quieted him. Neither man said anything else. She kept her eyes glued to a knot in the wood floor. "I appreciate your hospitality. If you could just tell me where my clothes are, I'll leave."

Tears burned in the back of her eyes, but she didn't dare look at the two men. She'd lose it completely if she did. Never before had she met such caring, compassionate and tender men in her life. Too bad they couldn't treat each other with the same caring and compassion she received from them. Love shouldn't come with a fist attached.

"Gillian, sit down." The sound of wood scraping on wood filled the silence in the room and gentle hands wrapped around her shoulders, steering her toward the chair. "Please?"

Before Ronan could seat her, she buried her face in his chest, sobbing into his shirt. She didn't want to leave, didn't want to walk out into the cold, to her death. But she couldn't stay and watch them tear each other apart either. Max had said they wouldn't be mad and yet the three men had argued. She presumed it had been about her.

Once she started, tear after tear poured from her eyes, her body wracked with sobs. She cried for every beating Kyle had given her, for every scrape on her body from her trek through the snow and for every piece of her heart she'd already given the three brothers. Ronan pressed his lips to her temple before her feet left the ground. The trust she had in him prevented her from squealing as she had every time before.

Instead, she wrapped her arms around his neck, pulling closer to him as he settled her on his lap. One hand stroked her head, while the other stroked her thigh and hip. The addition of two more hands didn't startle her a bit. She assumed Max had joined in comforting her.

God, she'd turned into a weepy female, the worst kind of woman according to her mother. Drying her eyes on Ronan's shirt, she looked from one set of concerned eyes to another.

"I really am leaving."

"No, you're not." Would Ronan always argue, she wondered.

"Max said you wouldn't be angry, but you three were shouting." Fiery heat burned her face and she imagined the blush covering her cheeks could light her way at night. "I can't stay and tear you three apart and I can't seem to not want," Lord, let the floor swallow her whole before she admitted her feelings, "to touch all three of you." *Too late.*

Max leaned forward and pressed a soft kiss to the tip of her nose before he spoke.

"We weren't arguing. Well, we were, but not for the reason you think. Conner thought you and I had gone farther than we did and he thought I'd broken a promise. That's why he was angry, poppet. He's also jealous as hell."

"All three of us care for you, Gillian. I told you all this last night, remember?"

As if she could forget. But Conner? Jealous? She licked her lips and felt Ronan's cock twitch beneath her and she thought she heard Max groan. But, it could have been the house settling. Sure.

"I don't want to drive a wedge between you three."

"You won't," they said in unison, their hands rubbing what she supposed they thought were soothing circles on her body. All their touch served to do was cause her arousal to blossom anew.

Turning to look into Ronan's eyes, she asked the question sure to cause her a premature death by mortification, but the question had to be asked.

"So, you're not angry that Max and I…"

"What did you and Max do, Gilly?" Ronan's voice was but a whisper as he leaned closer. For a second she thought he'd kiss her, but he nuzzled her cheek and neck instead, his unshaven cheek scratching and teasing her skin.

Max opened his mouth to speak, but one stern look from Ronan had him snapping his mouth shut. She wondered if she could learn to give those same looks. They could be useful.

"Gilly?"

Oh, damn. She'd hoped he had forgotten his question.

"Max, uh, he, um…" Gillian took a deep breath, before she told Ronan what they'd done. "Max sort of tore my pants and he kissed me, you know, *there*."

"That's all?"

She buried her face against his chest and nodded. Yep, death by embarrassment could come any minute now.

Ronan pressed his lips to her temple and whispered against her skin, his breath fanning and warming the side of her face, causing a shiver.

"There's nothing wrong with what you did with Max, Gilly. Nothing at all. I'm just jealous, and I have a feeling Conner is even more so since he hasn't touched you at all. He hasn't gotten a kiss, or gotten to taste your sweet cream. That's what we fought about, Gillian. Conner wants to make sure we don't take advantage of you or force you to do anything you don't want, *and* he's cranky because he hasn't spent much time with you alone."

"Oh. Lord, take me now."

Suddenly, she was lifted into Max's arms and thrown over his shoulder with a smack to her ass. This time, she did squeal, like a pig. Thumping her fists to his lower back, she screamed at him.

"What are you doing?"

"You said 'take me now', so I'm taking you. Where do you want to go? The bedroom?" Max brought one hand up and squeezed her ass, causing her to wiggle and squeal again. Part of her wanted to scream "yes", while the other knew there were some things still to be sorted out. Most importantly, Gillian wanted to know if Ronan had spoken the truth and there seemed to only be one way to figure out if he had.

"How about wherever Conner is?"

Her question must have stolen the wind from his sails. He pulled her off his shoulder, seating her on the kitchen table.

"He's still pretty riled, Gilly, you sure you want to go see him now? You can wait till he's calmed down…"

"Nope. Ronan, you got me some new clothes in town, right?"

"Yeah," he grumbled. He didn't seem to like her idea any better than Max. Too bad.

"Well, give me my new clothes and point me in the right direction."

"You sure about this, Gilly?"

"Yes, I'm sure. If he's not mad at me and only upset because we haven't spent time alone together, well, this is his chance to say so and get some." Lord, did she just say that? "TIME! It's his chance to get some time."

Chapter Eight

Dressed in her new jeans, layered flannel shirts, jacket and boots, Gillian set off into the snow-covered wilderness, leaving two very unhappy men behind. They'd pointed her in the right direction, mumbling about being careful and to stay on the path, the whole time looking like little kids who'd had their candy stolen. Tough, it was high time she made decisions for herself and got used to confrontation. It seemed her life with these three men would be full of it.

The thought made her stop dead in her tracks and lean against a tree. Had her thoughts really wandered there? Was she considering *staying* with the three brothers? No. Good, moral women didn't do things like live and love three men. *Love?* No, it wasn't love either. Affection, maybe. Like, and a connection, sure. But love? Nope, it was too soon to be love.

She wasn't trudging through the snow, opening her body up to new aches and pains for love. She wanted to make sure Conner wasn't mad and was okay. And maybe spend some time with him alone to see if they had a connection like she did with Ronan and Max. *Damn.* She really must have a "slut" tattoo somewhere on her body.

Gillian pushed away from the tree, continuing her journey to God only knew where. They'd told her it was a few hundred yards away, but she felt like she'd walked that far and a few thousand more. Oh well. One foot in front of the other—she'd done it before—she trudged through the snow-filled mud. At least this time, her body wasn't wracked with shivers and shooting pains as she walked. The clothes Conner and Ronan had purchased kept her body relatively warm and comfortable, even in the freezing temperatures.

Eyes glued to the ground, searching for the trail the brothers had convinced her could easily be seen, she ran straight into a tree, bumping her head on the trunk. The collision knocked her flat on her ass. She landed with a grunt.

So much for following the path.

She wiped the snow and bark debris from her hair, her fingers came away smeared in blood. Now they'd never let her out of the house by herself. After a few minutes, the bleeding seemed to stop and she hoisted her body from the ground. Ass soaked from sitting in the snow, she looked around, trying to find the trail. She couldn't see the "unmissable" trail, but could hear the gurgle of water in the distance. Hoping the sound came from the river the brothers had said Conner liked to sit near, she took off at a slow plod toward the noise.

Coming through the trees, she found Conner just where Ronan and Max said he would be—sitting on a twenty-foot high natural outcropping of rocks along the river's edge, staring into the water. The sound of the water muffled her approach, and he didn't turn to look at her until she'd nearly crawled onto the mound next to him. When he did notice her, he acted as if the world was coming to an end.

"Gillian! God! Are you okay?"

He jumped to his feet in one fluid movement and pulled her into his arms. The Bearclaw brothers sure did seem to have a thing with holding her. He lowered the two of them to the cold stone, cradling her weight in his lap. As soon as he'd settled her, he tugged off a glove and his cool fingers stroked the hair out of her eyes. She leaned into the touch, craving the feel of his skin against hers.

"Are you okay, Gillian? What happened, poppet?"

She sighed and let her eyes close as she snuggled closer to his warmth. She really did like his nickname for her.

"Nothing. Well, a tree sort of happened, but it doesn't matter. I wanted to come looking for you. I heard you three arguing, and I told Ronan and Max I wanted to leave…"

"You're not leaving."

His arms tightened around her. Smiling she looked into a pair of eyes which seemed so like Ronan and Max's, but different just the same.

"No, I'm not. At least, I'm not if I'm satisfied with our conversation."

Conner stiffened beneath her, it felt like she now sat on a wooden board instead of Conner's fleshy lap, but she snuggled closer, ignoring the tension humming through him. *Good, let him be the one on edge for once.*

"What do you want to know? What can I say to make you want to stay?"

"The truth. Nothing more than the truth."

"You might not like the truth, and then you'll leave."

She gazed at him and ran a finger down his cheek. His stubble scratched her skin and causing goose bumps to rise along her arm.

"Would you want to keep me with a lie?"

"No, of course not."

"Then trust me the way I've trusted the three of you for the past two days. Can you give me your trust, Conner?"

Instead of answering, he lowered his head to hers, brushing his lips in a soft sweet caress of skin against skin. His weather-cold lips warmed with each kiss. Infused with daring, she snaked her tongue out to slide along the seam of his lips, savoring his flavor as she begged for entrance. Conner obliged, spreading his heated lips he gave her free reign to explore the moist cavern of his mouth.

Gillian surged closer to Conner and slid her arms around his neck, tugging his chest to press against hers. *More.* She needed more. Sliding her hands beneath his jacket, she clutched his back ran her fingers over the taut, flannel-covered muscles.

Her tongue devoured Conner's mouth, licking and tasting his very essence; a mixture of hickory smoke and earth, musky and strong, like him. He moaned against her lips as she sucked his tongue, showing him others things she could do with her mouth, her lips.

She made sweeping, swirling motions in his mouth, teasing and dancing as they both fought for dominance. Each time she won, and she arched closer, pressed harder, demanding more.

Sliding her hands to his chest, she kneaded the tightened muscles, felt the tense jerks each time she sucked hard, and the delicate release of muscle as she released the suction. His cock, hard and thick seemed to reach for her body through the confines of his jeans and she did what she never thought she'd do.

She skimmed Conner's abdomen, stroking toward her destination. Her fingertips brushed the button of his jeans, the ice cold metal a stark contrast to the heat they had created. With one quick flick, the button was undone. A swift tug on the zipper and her fingers brushed the soft cotton of his underwear. Did he wear boxers or briefs? She'd soon know.

Tearing her mouth from his, their gazes met, a question visible in Conner's eyes.

"Let me." She breathed against his lips. A plea. She wanted to touch him, to feel his skin against hers, his shaft in her mouth. "Please."

Gillian wormed her hand into Conner's jeans, ignoring the tight squeeze, craving only to feel him in her hand, his arousal for her. He gasped against her mouth, his eyes squeezed shut when she managed to grasp his erection, her fingers not quite managing to envelope him fully. *Long and thick, mmm.*

"Questions." He moaned against her mouth just after she squeezed him. "You." *Pant.* "Had questions."

Gillian pulled back, flicking her tongue along his lower lip, teasing him. She didn't relinquish her hold on his cock, but gave him a bit of breathing room. Rubbing the tip of her nose against his, she whispered against his lips, anxious for his answers as she had plans for the cock in her hand. Never before had she ever felt so empowered, so free to do as she pleased. These three men wrenched those feelings out by showering her with freedom and caring.

"Were you angry for what I did with Max? Or Ronan? They said you were jealous, but not angry. Which was it?"

Conner closed his eyes and pressed his forehead to hers, and took a deep breath. "You want to talk about that now? Here? With your hand…"

Gillian tightened said hand and nodded. "Yes, here, now. Talk fast, make it good and I promise to make you a happy man."

Wow! Where had all this bravado and sexual aggression come from? Before meeting the three brothers' she'd been withdrawn, and always turned inward during sex, of any kind. Sex with Kyle had been when… *No.* She wouldn't think about that. Wouldn't think about the stench of alcohol on his breath, or what always managed to follow their "lovemaking". Not when she had another man's cock in her hand.

He moaned and sucked in a harsh breath, she slid her hand further into his pants, searching for his balls. "Both. Oh God, Gilly. Stop. Wait, don't stop." Her fingers found the tender skin where the skin of his shaft stretched lower and transformed to his sensitive scrotum.

"Both?" she queried, anxious to hear his explanation and get her lips around him. Scratching his skin through the fabric of his boxers, or maybe briefs, she waited for her answer.

"Both." His breath came in harsh pants, the sound warring with that of the river below. "Jealous. Wanted to be with you." Conner swallowed hard, his Adam's apple dancing along his throat. "Angry. Thought they took…" She tightened her grip, and taking advantage of the space she'd fought for in his pants, stroked him from balls to tip and back again. "Advantage." The word came out on a sigh, his breath fanning softly across the skin of her cheek.

So sweet, her Conner. So sweet and caring he'd nearly screamed the house down twice when he thought his brothers had taken advantage of her. First, when they'd just awoken, and again when he'd arrived home. While he had gotten angry unnecessarily both times, her heart melted for the man she held so near.

"They didn't take advantage, Conner."

He closed the distance between them, brushing his lips against hers. "No?"

"No."

Reaching the top of his underwear, she prayed her hand had warmed while buried within Conner's jeans. Slipping her fingers beneath the waistband, the feeling of silken steel against her palm sent a shiver through her body and Conner jerked in response.

Legs widening beneath her let Gillian slide to the ground beneath Conner's thighs, getting comfortable for what she had planned. Sitting on her heels, hand still buried and tight around his cock, she milked him softly as she tugged at his jeans and made more room.

"Gilly…"

"Mine, Conner. Save the protests for later."

Pulling the cotton fabric of his underwear down, she exposed his erection to the harsh winter winds.

"Fuck! It's cold!" he yelled, but didn't move to stop her. Obviously couldn't be too cold, Gillian thought with a secret smile.

The cinnamon-toned, mushroom-shaped head of his cock leaked droplets of pre-come that begged her mouth to taste. Leaning forward, she flicked the salty sweet fluid from his slit, rolling the bit of his essence around in her mouth. Going back for a second taste, she sucked the tip of his shaft into her mouth, running her tongue along the crown as she familiarized herself with his body.

His hand sifted through her curls, brushing them away so he could cup her cheek. Gillian froze under his caress. Her heart pounded as she waited for his next move, what his demand would be. Would he wrap his hand in her hair, forcing his cock down her throat? She waited for the tension, the pressure as he "guided" her to do his bidding, but it never came. His touch remained gentle and featherlight as she ventured to take more of him, never demanding she rush.

Willing her heart to calm, she inhaled a deep breath of the frost-laden air, begging her wayward thoughts to cease. Conner wasn't Kyle. Period. She needed to remember the distinction.

Widening her mouth, she slid further down Conner's pulsing shaft, slicking him with her saliva as she endeavored to take him fully. His moan of appreciation could be felt through her body; nothing existed for her but him at the moment, him and his cock. Tapping her tongue along his erection, she raised and lowered her head, riding his cock with her mouth, doing her best to grant him pleasure. His hand remained light, cupping her face, his thumb drawing circles on her cheekbone as she sucked him. She moaned around his cock and her pussy grew damp with each flick, lick, and suck she gave.

Conner's hips thrust his cock further into her mouth, and she swallowed convulsively around him as the head nudged the back of her throat. She wanted it all, wanted him all. The wind whipped and whirled around them, sprinkling snow over their bodies, but her thoughts and actions were focused on giving him pleasure.

Resting her hands on his hips, she inhaled, savoring the musky scent of arousal and sex emanating from Conner, and unable to help herself, moaned again. Increasing her suction, she milked his cock with her mouth, begging…no, demanding from him his release. In her mind she imagined him filling her mouth with the salty-sweet tang of his very essence, and she craved it; wanted to swallow every drop he'd give.

Her mouth stroked his staff as she teased and tempted his orgasm from him. She had a feeling he'd come soon—his moans came more frequently, as did his gasps. Gillian upped her tempo, sliding her lips and tongue over his saliva-slicked shaft, doing all she could to coax his warm seed to be released.

She sought out every vein and ridge of his erection, flicking over and over the places she found to be most tender and cause the greatest reaction. If he sucked in a breath, she flicked. If he groaned, she licked. And if he swore her name, she sucked the spot, aching to hear him scream again.

Her ministrations were soon rewarded, the combination of licking, flicking and sucking pushing him over the edge. His body tightened beneath her hands, hips jerking as he roared her name, his cock pulsing to life within the deep recesses of her mouth. Searing hot seed burst from the tip of his cock, filling her mouth as she'd hoped. The salty, musky taste of Conner's very essence seeped into her, sliding down her throat as she swallowed around him, savoring every drop her gifted her.

Releasing Conner's deflating shaft with a soft pop, she slid his underwear back in place before folding the flaps of his jeans over him, placing a soft kiss on the material.

Sitting back on her heels, more than satisfied with her performance, she accepted Conner's soft, sweet kisses he rained on her face, neck and lips. Pressing his face to her neck, sliding her fingers through his midnight locks, she wasn't expecting a large, dark moving object near the tree line to catch her eye. As it trudged through the falling snow, her interest piqued and she kept her eyes trained on the object. It slowly came into focus as it stepped out of the shadows and into the clearing. Gillian's heart froze and breath caught—a bear.

Chapter Nine

The trudge from her and Conner's "mountain" back to the cabin took longer than Gillian would have liked. True to form, Conner wouldn't let her walk and insisted on carrying her the entire way. He didn't seem concerned by the bear's appearance and had only increased his pace at her urging. While Gillian trusted Conner to know how to get back to the cabin, she kept her eyes peeled for any sign of the great big bear following them, waiting for its chance to pounce. Convinced the animal lurked in the shadows and behind every tree, her heart didn't calm until Conner placed her on the cabin's back porch.

When the back door opened, revealing Max, she dashed past him into the house, anxious to wrap herself in the protection the cabin offered.

"Shut the door, Max! There's a bear!"

He seemed as unconcerned as Conner, closing the door with a soft click as he stared at her, brow furrowed. "A bear?"

"Where's Ronan?" Conner looked around the room, causing Gillian to do the same.

"Um, out?" Max replied, not looking at either of them, but finding something on the floor very interesting.

Oh, God. Ronan had gone outside…with the bear!

"Do you two have guns? You should go get guns and save Ronan from the bear." When neither of the men moved, she urged them further. "Go! Ronan's your brother and he's in trouble and…"

"Oh. Who's in trouble dear?" A short, rotund woman with cinnamon skin and deep black hair stepped from the kitchen, dishcloth in hand. "Are you boys scaring this dear child?"

Conner's exclamation of "Mom!" was drowned out by Max's reassurance of "No, Mom". *Mom.* Good Lord, now she was meeting their mother. The slut-of-the-universe in the same room as the mother of the men who'd turned her into said slut. Lord, strike her down now and make it quick.

Shocked speechless, she let Conner mumble introductions. When their mother, who she now knew as Ethel, embraced her, she distractedly patted the woman's back as she shot panicked looks at Conner and Max of her shoulder. Couldn't they do something? Why had they not told her their mother was coming to visit? Not that she truly had any place with them other than a woman who liked to give and receive oral sex, but…damn it! Somebody should have said *something!*

Clearing his throat, Conner spoke up after introductions had been made. "Um, *Mom,* this is a surprise." He shoved his hands in his pockets, reminding her of a small child who'd been caught doing something they shouldn't. "You didn't call or anything. What brings you here? I assume you brought Dad?"

Ethel, with one arm slung around Gillian's waist, turned back toward the kitchen, dragging her along. "I had a dream that my boys needed me, so here I am. Why don't you two leave us ladies to dinner and go help Father and Dad with Gillian's car? I heard Father cursing up a storm, and I could hear Dad laughing like a damned hyena."

Gillian gave Conner and Max a pleading look, but both men shrugged their shoulders as if powerless against the vibrant storm that was Ethel.

At least Max tried. "Um, Mom, we can introduce Gilly to…"

"Nonsense. You boys go on outside and let everyone know dinner will be ready shortly. Gilly and I have some talking to do and its best done without the 'men' of the family hanging around. Now, out with the two of you."

No. Not out. Please not out. Maybe Gillian was the only one who remembered the bear lurking in the snow. Bears were big and strong with massive teeth, which could rip a person to shreds. Why weren't they afraid?

"Um, what about the bear, Mrs. Bearclaw?"

Ethel patted her arm. "Now, don't you worry about the bear. The bear wouldn't *dare* come near the house, or I'll have something to say about it. Didn't I tell you to call me Ethel, dear?"

Ethel's kind blue eyes, so similar to Max's, met hers and Gillian felt some of her tension flow from her body—as if a simple look from their mother could ease her fears and calm her.

Conner tried one last time to get Gillian out of the situation she found herself in. "Mom, we can…"

"It's okay, Conner," she stopped his plea before he could finish. Maybe getting to know the woman who had raised the three men she'd been spending time with would be a good thing. "I'll be fine, and if your mom says you'll be safe outside, then I guess you will. But, please be careful."

"You sure, poppet?" She wanted to run and jump into his arms and shower him with kisses. His nickname for her gave Gillian the deep down warm-fuzzies like nothing else.

"I'm sure." Smiling, she walked with Ethel into the kitchen, leaving two of her three men standing in the hallway.

Settling at the kitchen table, she watched Ethel check the pots on the stove, adding pinches of this and that to several of them before she sat across from her. Just as Ethel opened her mouth to speak, Ronan stomped through the back door. Ethel stood so fast, her chair nearly toppled backwards.

"Ronan!" Swiveling in her chair, Gillian was surprised to see Ronan frozen in the doorway, half naked and pale as new fallen snow. "Ronan Bearclaw, so help me. If you were smaller I'd take you over my knee." Ethel stomped her foot. "Gillian said there was a *bear* outside. You wouldn't know anything about that, would you? Didn't run into any *bears* by chance?"

Ronan swallowed, Adam's apple bobbing. "No, ma'am."

"Hmph. Go get dressed, young man, and then help Pop chop some firewood." Ronan moved like lightning, dashing down the hallway as if the bear were on his heels. "And I better not hear of any 'bear' sightings, that clear?" Ethel yelled after him.

A muffled "Yes, ma'am" drifted back to them and Ethel plopped back into her chair.

Gillian's head spun with everything she'd heard. From the sounds of it, Ethel had arrived with three other people, but she couldn't determine who they were, not really.

"Now then, where were we? Have to get the 'woman's talk' out of the way before the boys and their fathers get back or we'll never have a chance to talk." The way Ethel spoke of her family, the warm smile and loving expression, showed Gillian she cared for the brother's and their...wait.

"Did you say fathers? As in plural? More than one?" She'd grown up being taught not to ask such personal questions, but she was pretty sure Ethel had said *fathers*.

"Why, yes, dear. That's what I wanted to tell you about before they came stomping through the house. I'm sure the boys haven't told you about our family's history, or you'd be on your honeymoon by now."

Gillian's head spun. "Wait. Start at the beginning."

Ethel reached across the table, covering Gillian's folded hands with her own. "Dear, let me start by saying that what you're feeling for my boys is natural. I could see it in the way my Conner carried you, the way Max stared out the window waiting for your return and the way Ronan turned into a bear...of a man without you. My husbands feel the same way for me, and I imagine my feelings for them are similar to what you're feeling for Conner, Max and Ronan right about now."

Gillian shook her head, unwilling to admit her feelings for the brothers to anyone. She still hadn't accepted them herself. Good women didn't go around fantasizing about having three men at once. They just didn't.

"It's hard to accept at first, I admit. Society doesn't look upon our relationship as a normal one, but in our tribe, it's as normal as a man marrying a woman. When identical twins or triplets are born, they are each part of the same soul. Our tribe believes that in order for the men, or women to be happy, they must find their true soul mate." Ethel shrugged slightly, "But how can identical siblings who share a soul find their soul mates when part of their own being is so intimately connected to their brother or sister? We believe that in order for them to be happy, the brothers must stay together and search for the one person who can complete and compliment them all."

Gillian's mouth went dry, her tongue sticking to the roof of her mouth. "You're saying…you're saying I'm their…"

"I believe you are, and I couldn't be happier. I have a feeling they believe you are as well, but they're afraid. But I didn't tell you this to frighten or burden you, dear. I just wanted to prepare you for the three hulking men who look a lot like the boys and will be joining us shortly. My sons won't rush you into anything; their fathers and I raised them better. But I also won't hide my love for my husbands, and I didn't want our behavior to shock you."

Tears burned Gillian's eyes. Their mother thought she was their soul mate and couldn't be happier. With a few chosen words and squeeze of Gillian's hands, Ethel had eased her fears about being in what society would deem a "perverted" relationship. Not holding them back, the salty fluid leaked from her eyes, streaming down her cheeks. Gillian wiped them away, drying her hands on her jeans.

Ethel clicked her tongue. "None of that, dear, none of that. No crying in heart-to-hearts. Dinner's about ready, and we'll have six hungry men descending on us in any second. Why don't you pop into the bathroom and wash up?"

With a nod, Gillian rose on shaky legs. Not questioning her need, she shuffled around the table to stand face-to-face with Ethel and enveloped the older woman in a tight hug. "Thank you."

"Oh no, dear. Thank *you*. You're perfect for my baby boys and they've been looking for you for so long. I meant what I said, you shouldn't allow yourself to be rushed, but I know the four of you will be very happy together."

Gillian had a feeling their mother was right. Pulling out of the hug with a sheepish smile, she padded down the hallway and into the bathroom, anxious to dash warm water on her face and clean up any remaining blood from the scratch on her head. She didn't think much remained, Max hadn't even seemed to notice the cut, but she didn't want to take any chances.

Running warm water in the sink, she splashed it over her face, wiping at the last remnants of blood along her hairline. With any luck, the other two wouldn't notice. Turning off the water and drying her face, she bent at the waist and crossed her arms before laying them on the cool counter top. Propping her chin on her arms, she closed her eyes, her mind rolling with the information Ethel had shared.

Three men and one woman? Wow, apparently in their tribe, such a relationship was viewed as normal. Gillian had never been one to believe in legends and soul mates, but she couldn't deny the feelings Ronan, Conner and Max elicited from her. A general sense of safety, along with warmth and protection enveloped her when in their presence. She didn't think anything bad could happen to her with them around.

Ethel seemed to think she was the missing piece of their foursome, but did Gillian feel the same way? Beyond a sexual attraction lurked other feelings she didn't know if she could release yet. She'd trusted once before and loved fully, only to be betrayed and nearly killed. Fear still lingered in Gillian's heart, but maybe it was time to release the fear and open up to them. They had proven their worth to her already. The least she could do was try.

Opening her eyes, another figure in the mirror captured her attention. Her heart stopped before picking up a galloping beat and fear, deep seeded, physical beating imposed fear, held her in place.

"I've missed you." Kyle stepped closer, a mud-caked hand stroking the top of her head and still she didn't move. "I've been hunting you, and now I've found you." Thick, dirty fingers dug through her hair, snagged and pulled at the strands as he forced her head back as she stood, moving with his grasp. "You've been running a long time, Gillian. But I've found you, and now, I'll cleanse you before I take you back." His breathing came harsh. The stench nearly overwhelmed her and she opened her mouth to breathe. She could taste his hate in the air. "Got to wash those men off of you. You whored your body out to them, but I'll wash you clean again."

He yanked on her hair and toppled her backwards. She landed with a thud and a scream muffled by his hand over her mouth. His hand moved and closed around her throat, his grip tightening with each breath, cutting off her airflow.

"Ah, ah, ah. No screaming, Gillian. You remember our rule."

Of course, she remembered. *No screaming, no yelling, no fighting back. Lie there and take it, bitch.* She'd close her eyes and take it, take everything. Nodding, she sighed as he relaxed the hold he had on her throat.

"Gilly? You okay in there, dear?" *Damn, Ethel.* Ethel needed to run, to hide. He'd hurt her and Gillian would never forgive herself. Never.

His voice grated in her ear. "Get rid of her."

Good, he didn't want Ethel, only her. "I'm fine, Ethel, just tripped and I'm having a bit of trouble with a *door*."

"All right dear. If you're sure?"

"I'm fine, Ethel, really. Just trouble with a *door* and then I'll be out." *Please let him be too drunk to realize what I'm trying to say. Please.*

Kyle yanked on her hair again and she followed his tugs, bending at the waist as he dragged her toward the bathroom window. Pulling a gun from his waistband, she eyed the barrel as he directed her with harsh roughened whispers. "Out. Don't yell for help. I'd hate to shoot someone because you couldn't remember our rule."

She'd hate that too. After climbing through the window, she made sure each step she made left large, deep prints in the snow. Maybe they could follow them and rescue… No, they'd only get hurt. Gillian couldn't stand the thought of them getting hurt. She'd have to figure a way out of this on her own. She'd escape and come back to them. She would.

The gun pressed into her back as she stumbled through the woods, her adrenaline pumping, and her muscles ready and waiting to be put into use. She'd act docile and wait. Wait for the perfect moment to run, hit, or hide.

The sound of rushing water filtered through the trees and Eric's previous words came back in a rush. *I'll cleanse you before I take you back. No!* Her mind screamed, and her body rebelled. She stopped moving, frozen to the spot. Instinct told her he planned to use the river as his cleansing medium. There was no way she'd go willingly into the frozen waters of the river. No.

"Move." He cocked the gun, the bullet dropped into place as he prepared to shoot it into her body. "Move your ass." Kyle shoved the barrel into her spine, digging into her through her layers of clothing.

Death by beating and Kyle's version of cleansing or hypothermia, which should she choose? Neither sounded appealing, but the water—it moved fast, deadly cold. It would sweep her away. Maybe…maybe she could swim to safety—dive into the freezing, turgid waters and let the current carry her away from him, away from danger.

Stars burst behind her eyes as something hard, cold crashed into her temple. Pain lit every nerve ending and she stumbled, catching herself on a tree. The bark dug into her palms, but the extra twinge kept her coherent while Kyle barked orders at her. "Move." He struck her with the butt of the gun. "Your." This time, he punched her in the stomach and she slid down the trunk. "Ass." She hadn't seen it coming and wasn't prepared for the kick. His foot struck her ribs and what little air she'd sucked in rushed out with a wheeze.

Kyle didn't give her time to recover though. He dug his fingers into her hair, grabbed a handful and yanked. She had no choice but to follow. Gillian stumbled to her feet, tripping on twigs and rocks as she followed Kyle's path. Bent over at the waist, she still couldn't catch her breath. Tiny droplets of blood stained the snow beneath her and she prayed the brothers wouldn't see. She didn't want them following, not when Kyle had a gun. And he'd use it.

They'd reached the bank of the river, and Kyle threw her as he released his grip. Gillian took a step forward, choosing her fate. She'd get away and begin her run again. As much as she wanted to return to her three men, she couldn't risk bringing this danger upon them again.

Chapter Ten

Warmth surrounded her. A dull ache throbbed through her body, but the warmth kept it mostly at bay. Sweet, tender heat enveloped her from head to toe. With heavy eyelids, she awakened to her room. *Hmmm...* Even in death she dreamt of her place with the Bearclaw brothers. Ironic. She should have told them of her growing feelings for them before she died, should have confessed to her attraction to the three of them. Too late now.

With a sigh, she rolled to her side and the ache increased for a moment, transforming to a shooting pain which covered her completely before resuming its previous dull throb. *Damn*, heaven had been touted as the perfect place, so why did it hurt so much? The warmth shifted behind her, covering her now exposed back and she settled back into her peaceful sleep, dreaming of the three men she had left behind.

Time passed as she continued to rest, semi-waking occasionally to find the same heat surrounding her, infusing her with feelings of love and protection as she slept. She imagined sleeping with the Bearclaw brothers would feel like this—protected from all sides, cared for and loved like no other. Part of her wondered if God would let her go back, go back to her men and profess her feelings. After staring into Kyle's hate-filled gaze, she realized her feelings for Ronan, Conner and Max had to surely be love.

She grew restless, light burned through her eyelids, and she threw an arm over her face to block out the morning sun. Her other arm came into contact with a large, warm body. Jerking awake, she went rigid with the realization that she wasn't alone.

"Gilly?" *Ronan.*

She'd been sent to hell. Nowhere else would phantasms of her loves be presented to torment her. Whimpering, she covered her face, tears burning and soaking the sheets as she cried.

"Poppet?" *God, not Conner, too.*

The devil was cruel, creating creatures similar to two of her loves. Would Max round out the threesome?

"No." *Please no.*

"No what, Gilly? You need something, love?" She needed to be alive, not trapped in hell with Ronan and Conner.

Unseen hands tugged at the sheet covering her face and she relinquished it reluctantly. Gillian squeezed her eyes shut, tight. She hadn't expected the warm, callused hand stroking her face, or the silken lips kissing away her tears. The apparitions kissed a dead woman and the pain nearly tore her apart.

"Dead," she croaked. Her voice sounded harsh.

"No one's dead, poppet. You came close, but you seem to be doing well now," Conner whispered against her cheek.

"Don't lie." Gillian didn't have the strength to say much else, but she didn't dare hope the specter spoke the truth. Because if it did, it meant she wasn't too late. She could confess her feelings and open her arms to them. If…

"Not a lie, Gilly. Never a lie. You were in bad shape when Dad pulled you from the river, but Mom fixed you up right. Your body is probably sore from banging on the rocks and from…from the beating Kyle gave you, but you are alive, my Gilly," Ronan's voice assured her, his lips brushing her ear with every word.

Alive? She lived? Not a lie? Not hell. Not illusions. Alive. God, she wanted to dance and sing and hug the men beside her, but she didn't have the strength.

Snippets of her memory came filtering back as she lay on the bed, wrapped in the warmth of Conner and Ronan's bodies. Images of Kyle beating her, striking her as he pushed her toward the water filtered through. The butt of the gun had struck her once…no, twice, at her temple. Had she said something to make him angry? She couldn't remember. But he wanted her clean, cleansed.

Gun cocked, ready to shoot, he'd pushed her toward the water. It had been her chance. Instead of stepping in slowly like he'd no doubt expected, she jumped, not thinking of the way the ice cold water would freeze her muscles, tighten her body. Once wrapped in the river's embrace, she had been powerless to direct her body's movement. A victim of the roaring current, it swept her downstream, leaving a raging Kyle behind.

She remembered hearing screams and shouts. The echo of gunshots flittered through her mind. Had she been shot? No. Conner and Ronan hadn't mentioned her being shot. What about…

"Max?" Her eyes traveled from Conner to Ronan and back again, and she didn't think she would like what she was about to hear. Their faces paled slightly, brows furrowed as if thinking of a lie to tell her. "The truth."

As if conjured by the mention of his name, Max's voice traveled through the silent room to capture her attention. "She's awake? Oh, Gilly…"

Levering her body up, she rested her weight on her elbows as she stared at Max in the doorway. A white bandage wrapped around his head as well as a sling cradling his right arm told her that if anyone had been shot, it had been Max. Her carefree, smiling, mischievous Max. A sob tore at her throat, but she swallowed it back. No matter what she'd been through, it was obvious he'd been through worse.

"No tears, Gilly. I'm okay and so are you." He closed the distance between them. Conner rose, giving Max his place. The moment Max settled on the bed, she laid her head in his lap, anxious to feel his touch. His hand stroked through her hair and pulled at the tangled strands, but the sharp tugs of pain reminded her she was alive. She didn't complain.

"What happened?" She had to know. Had to know how they knew she needed them and they came to her rescue.

"Maybe we could talk about this another…" Max tried to push it off, but she needed to know.

"Now."

The three men sighed in unison and she imagined them sharing a look of annoyance, but it didn't matter to her.

"Poppet?" Conner hedged.

"Now, please now." She gripped Max's thigh, afraid he'd disappear and not give her the answers she needed.

Ronan pressed against her back, his chest, groin and thighs melding to her. Conner laid on the bed near her feet, but in her line of sight. Surrounded. Her men surrounded her, each of them stroking a part of her with gentle touches.

Max spoke first. "We came in after fixing your car and Mom said you'd been in the bathroom a while. At first…at first, we thought she'd told you more about us than we would have liked and you were hiding out. We got pissed and argued." Gillian smiled as she twined her fingers with Ronan's on her hip. She just bet they argued. "Then she mentioned that maybe you were stuck. You said you were having trouble with a door."

Ronan's fingers tightened around hers, he growled in her ear. "We knew he had you. God, we ran harder and faster than we ever had before. Broke the door down and saw his footprints on the floor." It figured Ronan would notice the footprints. "I followed through the window, running, needing to find you. Max was on my heels, Conner got our dads. By the time we caught up to you and Kyle, you'd already thrown yourself into the river. I…I tried to come in after you, but it swept you away…" Hot, wet tears fell onto her cheek and she realized what her life meant to them. She'd been willing to end her life to save them and he'd been willing to do the same.

Max brushed the hair from her face. She looked up into his eyes. "I fought him. He ran, up the outcropping, firing at me, but I didn't care. I thought he'd…he'd hurt you, killed you. Before I could get to him, he fell over the edge and into the river. Still firing as he went in."

The tension in the room rose, thrumming through the brothers. Conner stroked the tender skin of her ankle, drawing her attention. "Dad and I found you, floating, near frozen. We pulled you…" His grip tightened as he drew a breath. "Pulled you from the river, stripped you and wrapped you in our jackets, brought you home." They'd brought her home. Home. She liked the sound of that word. "Mom took care of you, told us what to do. We wanted to take you to a hospital, but Mom said your spirit is strong." Conner gifted her with a half smile. "She was right."

"I said her spirit was strong, but her body is not invincible!" The four of them jumped, jostling Max and sending new aches through her body. Ethel, framed by the doorway with three large men crowded behind her, stomped her foot. "Leave the girl to rest."

"Aw, Mom," the three men groaned in unison.

Conner spoke up for them, trying to cajole their mother and fathers. "Please?"

Fathers, wow. Staring at the men standing behind the diminutive Ethel, Gillian saw where the brothers' size came from. At least now she had a good idea of what her men would look like in about thirty years.

Ethel stomped forward, an imposing presence even if the only reason she towered over the men was because they were lying down. "She needs her rest and so does your brother, Conner Bearclaw."

"Pop?" Max whined. A thirty-year-old man, whining.

"You heard your mother," one of their fathers spoke. Gillian could hardly keep the brothers straight in her mind, how would she differentiate their fathers? Then again, when had she decided she would stay? *When I thought I'd died and lost my chance. No chickening out now.*

"Father…" Ronan pleaded. At least now she knew what the references to Pop, Father and Dad were. It was how the family differentiated between the different fathers. Good idea, she'd have to remember that when she…

"Now, Ronan," another father replied. They all looked the same! Dammit! Midnight black hair, brown eyes, and the cinnamon skin of their ancestors—and all three of them wore large grins as the brothers tried to weasel their way into staying.

"Will you boys stop?" Ethel's smile belied her stern tone. "I swear, you three are like newborn cubs, just begging to play in the snow." Shaking her head, she turned back toward the bedroom door, accepting defeat. Before stepping over the threshold, she turned back and issued a warning. "You let her *rest*, you hear? Your fathers and I are going into town to deal with the sheriff and I imagine we'll be bringing them back with us. They'll want to talk to her and the three of you, so relax and rebuild your strength."

Ethel left them, her husbands trailing behind. For such large men, they seemed like meek puppy dogs in her presence. The thought brought bubbling laughter to the surface and she couldn't contain it. Chuckling, shaking against the three men, she laughed.

"What's so funny?" Ronan growled, nipping her ear.

"Your dads, I was thinking that they act like little puppy dogs with your mom."

"Puppy dogs? No, I think of them as acting like newborn cubs following their momma." Max weighed in, a twinkle in his eye.

"Cubs? As in bears? What's with all the bear references in this family? Is it because you live on a mountain and they're all over the place?"

"Yeah, that's it," Conner answered, his mouth hovering over her toes. She held her breath, hoping, praying he'd taste her. For some reason, the desire to feel his mouth on her was nearly overwhelming.

Chapter Eleven

Gillian nudged her foot closer to him, an involuntary action. Or was it? The cause didn't seem to matter, as the effect was Conner lowering his lips, opening his mouth and snaking his tongue out to flick between her toes. A rapid beat tapped out on the sensitive skin, like a hummingbird's wings. Eyes drifting close, she moaned as he slid his hands over her ankles and calves, the calluses scratching and waking her skin.

The scent of hickory smoke and earthy musk teased her nostrils, distracting her from Conner's caresses. Seeking out the source, she nuzzled Max's groin, causing him to moan.

"Shouldn't, Gilly," Max groaned, her teeth found his cotton covered, hardened cock. "Really shouldn't."

"Want to," she whispered against his groin, exhaling her hot, moist breath against the aroused skin. With trembling hands, she fumbled with the waistband of his shorts, tugging at the elastic until Max relented and shucked the shorts himself before settling on the bed again.

Mouth searching, her tongue flicked the newly formed drop of pre-come from the tip of his shaft. Max's essence held a lighter, sweeter flavor than Conner's and she wanted more. Shutting out the other two men, she focused solely on Max. Propping her body on one elbow, she leaned over his waist, sliding her mouth up and down his shaft, sucking the ridged skin.

"Good. So good, Gilly," Max praised her. And like Conner, he rested one hand on the side of her face, stroking his callused fingers over her skin, sending shivers through her body. She needed more, needed to be touched everywhere.

As if reading her mind, sensing her desire, Ronan's hand slid from her hip to center over her hair-dusted mound. Shifting, she opened her legs for him, sending up a silent "thank you" that no one had bothered to redress her. Ronan's fingers sifted through her curls, delving between her lips and finding her clit with unerring accuracy. He began slowly, circling the tiny nub in time with her sucking of Max. If she increased her pace, he did. If she slowed, he followed her lead.

Gillian's pussy clenched and ached, leaking juices, lubricating her body in preparation…for what? Neither man had taken things further. She opened her eyes and sent a pleading look to Max.

"Need more, Gilly?"

She whimpered around his cock, wrapping her fingers around the base of his shaft, she prayed her understood her need.

"Need to be fucked, Gilly?"

Eye fluttering close, she moaned around his erection. He had understood and maybe she'd get what she needed. She'd almost lost her chance with the three men surrounding her and she wanted, needed to reconnect. Pussy weeping in anticipation, she didn't fight Ronan as he raised her leg, draping it over his thigh.

When the tip of his cock probed her opening, she arched her back inviting him in. Ronan slid the tip into her heat, stretching her core with the tiny bit he'd given her. She knew the men were long and thick, she hadn't thought about what it would feel like to make love to all three of them at the same time. His girth stretched her wide, almost to the point of pain. He gripped her hip tight as he slid more of his length into her cunt. It rippled and clenched around him, she needed it all.

In one final thrust, he seated his cock fully into her pussy, causing her to gasp around Max's cock, pulling it free of her mouth. "Fuck!"

Breath panting, she worked her hand along Max's shaft as Ronan remained motionless inside of her.

"So hot, so tight, Gilly," Ronan gritted out between clenched teeth.

Squeezing the cock in her hand, she enveloped Max again, now used to Ronan's invading cock and the way it stretched and filled her so completely. Sliding up and down, she felt the bed shift, but ignored it. With four bodies on a bed, there was no telling...

A soft flicker. A butterfly's caress, wafted over her clit, causing her eyes to burst open again and meet Max's. "Just Conner getting a taste, Gilly."

Conner licked her pussy from where Ronan thrust to her clit and back again. Gillian spread her legs further, opening her body to Ronan and Conner, silently pleading with them to love her. They obliged.

Conner's tongue circled her clit, flicking the aroused nubbin, pulling her orgasm closer with each lick. Lazily, she continued to suck Max, but her mind remained focused on what was being done to her body. Max didn't seem to mind, his moans assuring her that even an unfocused blow job was enjoyable.

Her arousal grew with each thrust of Ronan's cock into her pussy. Gillian's walls clasped around him, tightening with each deep thrust. Arching her back, she rocked her body with him, alternatively pressing her hips closer to Conner's mouth and Ronan's cock. More, she needed and craved more.

A callused hand stroked her breast, tweaking one nipple. Max. She moaned her appreciation, earning her a gasp in return. He liked her moans.

Ronan increased his pace, either sensing her need or approaching his own release, she didn't know. But she reveled in the added sensations. His breath came in harsh pants, fingers digging into her hip as he neared completion. God, her own orgasm was close. So close.

Conner swirled his tongue around her nubbin before wrapping his lips around the small bit of nerve-filled flesh. He sucked the small protrusion, sending her screaming toward release. The thrusting of Ronan's cock combined with Conner's tongue and mouth sent her careening over the edge, coming in a series of spasms. Her pussy tightened around Ronan's cock, rippling with each wave of her orgasm as it washed over her, presumably triggering his own. He roared with his release, body tightening behind her as a few jerked thrusts pronounced the bursts of his seed from his body.

Max wasn't far behind, as if their orgasms triggered his own, his seed flowed from the tip of his cock and down her throat. The musky sweet flavor burst on her taste buds as she swallowed every bit of seed he gifted her with, relishing in what she could draw from her men. But one of her men hadn't found his release, hadn't gained any pleasure while pleasuring her.

Releasing Max's now flaccid cock with a soft plop, she licked the last evidence of his release from his skin before focusing her gaze on Conner, still nestled between her legs.

Max rose on shaky legs and snatched his discarded shorts from the floor before settling on a nearby chair, leaving the area near her head free.

"Conner?" Gillian tilted her head in invitation. With Ronan's cock still deeply embedded in her pussy, she couldn't exactly get up and crawl over to him. Besides, Ronan's cock was still half-hard within her. The feeling of being so completely filled sent a newly blooming arousal humming through her veins.

Conner didn't answer, didn't move, at first. He rolled from the bed, stripping his body bare under her gaze, before crawling to lie in front of her. She pressed forward, skimming his chest with her breasts, shivering at the touch of his steel cock against her stomach. His hand skimmed the skin of her hip, following her leg until his fingers grasped her knee. Shifting her leg to his desire, he dislodged Ronan's cock, quickly, with one large thrust, replacing it with his own.

He rolled to his back, pulling her with him until she straddled his hips, his pulsing cock buried deep within her heat. Gillian froze, now the center of attention, she didn't know how to act, what to do.

As if sensing her problem, Conner reassured her. "Ride me, poppet. Let them watch you ride me."

Conner's hands slid along her thighs and he gripped the globes of her ass, running his fingertips along her crease. She rose, sliding up his cock, before sinking down again. Conner moaned, his body arching toward her. She did it again; rose and fell over him, smiling with each sound she pulled from him.

Continuously, she rode him, moving along his erection, her arousal burning anew. Conner's juice slicked fingers teased her back entrance, rimming the tiny pucker, arousing her further. She'd never taken anyone there, but with three men and one woman… It would be inevitable. The thought brought her orgasm closer, burning the edges of her consciousness as it ran rampant through her body.

When he slid a finger into her anus, she cried out. The sensations of the never-touched nerve endings firing to life nearly burned her alive. She increased her tempo, chasing her release and demanding Conner's. Again, she'd come again with a man buried deep within her pussy. Not just any man, one of her men.

Whimpering, focusing on achieving her orgasm, she didn't notice her other two men had moved. They'd joined them on the bed. Ronan teased her nipples, stroking her breasts, fondling the aching orbs as she rode his brother.

Max slid his hand down Gillian's abdomen, resting above her mound. He applied additional pressure to her mound, just above her clit so with each descent, additional zings of pleasure shot through her body. These things combined pushed her closer to completion, but it was their words, which brought her closer to the edge.

Ronan's husky growl echoed in her ears. "Fuck him. Fuck him good and hard and come on his cock, Gillian. Come for us, baby."

She gasped, the words sinking through her body as she rode Conner.

"Harder. Fuck that cock harder, Gilly. Come all over his cock. Want to hear you scream with it," Max whispered in her ear.

Eyes closing, she concentrated on the hands on her body, the cock within her heat. So close, so damn close. She'd never come more than once during sex, but she wanted to this time, needed to. Not just for herself, she wanted to gift her men, give them what they desired.

Conner's voice, strained and tight, pushed her over the edge, throwing her headlong into her most powerful orgasm yet. "Come on my cock. Want to feel you come around me, poppet."

"Fuck!" she screamed. As her pussy convulsed, tremors traveled through her body as every nerve snapped to life at once. The orgasm washed through her body in giant waves, her muscles tensing and releasing with each new surge. The brothers whispered words of approval, lost in the harsh pants.

Conner stiffened beneath her, his hips surging toward her as he found his own release. Gripping him beneath her, she held fast, wanting every drop of his seed to remain locked within. As he relaxed into the bed, she did the same, resting her weight on Conner and leaning against Ronan's chest. Not wanting to leave Max out of their moment, she slid her hand down her abdomen and laced their fingers together.

The sounds of their breathing slowed, to soft gasps as they each calmed, until silence reigned. Gillian was the first to break it.

Pulling away from Ronan and releasing Max's hand, she braced her hands on Conner's chest, preparing to rise from his body.

"Shower. Now."

Ronan saved her the trouble of a slow, aching withdrawal; he scooped her into his arms and leapt from the bed, laughing at her and Conner's groans. "Yeah, yeah. Come on, lazy bones, outta bed. I can't believe you made our woman do all the work."

Laughing, she draped her arms around Ronan's neck, inhaling his musky scent. She wondered what he would taste like. Would he have the same musky flavor with a hint of hickory or would he be darker? Accepting that the men were three parts of one whole, she knew they would all be similar, yet different and she couldn't wait to discern the differences between them.

Chapter Twelve

Dressed after their shower, Gillian, followed by her three men proceeded to the living room where Ethel, her husbands, and the police awaited. As she settled in a chair, her men to either side and behind, surrounding her. Touching their hands in reassurance, she answered each question posed by the police, cooperating fully.

Gillian detailed each instance of abuse she suffered at Kyle's hands before finally running in her desperation to get away from him. After running for days, he'd always managed to find her. The last time he found her, just before she'd stumbled upon the Bearclaws' cabin, he'd nearly choked her to death. She pulled her turtleneck sweater aside, revealing the still healing angry, purple bruises his hands had left.

Gillian's story jumped to Kyle's arrival at the Bearclaw cabin via breaking through a window and surprising her in the bathroom. He'd forced her, at gunpoint, to leave the house, urging her toward the river. At some point, beatings began and her memory became fuzzy. The one clear thought she had was of jumping into the river, in a desperate attempt to escape him.

The men added their bits and pieces to the story then, explaining their confrontation with Kyle and finding Gillian, bruised and unconscious downriver.

By the time the police left the cabin, they'd been satisfied that while Kyle had been guilty of numerous crimes, his death had been of his own making and Max was lucky to have gotten away with a simple gunshot wound to the shoulder. The search and rescue team found Kyle's body downstream, washed up on the bank. While Gillian was happy to be safe from him forever, she shivered at the memory of the freezing river. She wouldn't have wished such a death on anyone, even Kyle.

* * *

After a few days, Ethel, whom she affectionately called "Mom" and her three husbands, "Dad", "Pop", and "Father", left the four of them to return home. But not before giving Gillian instructions on how to care for Max's shoulder and giving the three brothers strict instructions on how gentle and *honest* they needed to be with Gillian. Gentle, Gillian could understand, but *honest?* What was that all about?

The moment Ethel and her husbands pulled out of the driveway, Gillian assumed they'd get back to the gentle touches and sexual exploration they'd started the week before. But they didn't. Instead, the brothers kept their distance. Confused, she assumed their reserved behavior resulted from their mother's warning. Brushing off their behavior, she had gone to bed, alone, but resolved to bring the four of them together again. The lovemaking they'd shared had been too monumental not to repeat.

The following morning, after waking alone in the guest bedroom, Gillian found out the meaning behind Ethel's instructions on honesty. Padding into the kitchen, Max plopped a heaping pile of French toast in front of her. Inhaling the sweet, cinnamon fragrance, she picked up her fork, prepared to dig in.

"Where are Ronan and Conner?" She shoved a forkful of the heated, egg-soaked bread into her mouth. It needed more syrup. Drizzling the sugary syrup on the slices, she topped it off with confectioner's sugar. *Perfect.*

"They're, um, out." Max turned from her and went to work cleaning the kitchen. Interesting, since she hadn't seen him cook or clean in the week and a half she'd known him. Make messes and not clean them up, sure. But never cook *and* clean up after himself. Something was going on.

Snagging a piece of bacon from a nearby plate, she crunched the crispy meat, chewing as she debated her next move. What were they up to? Not wanting to ruin their plans, she figured she'd play along, for now.

But she could still make him sweat, right? "When will they be back? Did they go to town?"

Max froze at the stove, dropping one of the pans back onto a burner. Wiping his hands on his pants, he answered Gillian. "Um, no. They…they just went out for a walk."

"A walk, huh? Wow. It's awfully cold for a walk," she deadpanned. Taking another bite of bacon, she washed it down with some orange juice, giving him a moment to formulate a response.

"Yeah, you know, a walk. They wanted to take a look around the property. With some coffee and a jacket, it's not too cold." He mumbled something else below his breath. She thought she heard the word "bear", but couldn't be sure.

Poking the man a little, she replied. "A walk? Maybe we should join them. I can be dressed in no time and…"

Max cut her off. "Perfect. Go get dressed and I'll get the coffee." It seemed as if a great weight had lifted from his shoulders at her suggestion.

Confused, she figured she'd continue to play along. What harm could it do? Finishing the remnants of her breakfast, she bounded from the chair, pressed a quick "thank you" kiss to Max's cheek and left him to get dressed.

Minutes later, thermos in hand, they stepped onto the porch. A gust of wind enveloped them, burrowing through her layers with ease. Shivering, she changed her mind. Let the men wander the snow and cold, she'd stay warm in the house until they returned, *thankyouverymuch*.

Opening her mouth to inform Max of her decision, she snapped it shut with a click of her teeth and mumbled through lips fear kept trapped together. "Bbbbear…"

Oh, God! Not just one…two! Two bears trundled from the forest and toward them. One slow, lumbering step at a time. Panicked, she dashed to the back door, anxious for the relative safety the cabin could provide. Max blocked her path, gripping her shoulders.

"Bears, Max! Bears!" *Idiot!* Didn't he see them, how could he not? They had to weigh nearly a ton each and they drew closer with each passing second. They'd be upon them at any moment. She didn't live through Kyle's attack to end up being some wild animal's dinner. Beating on Max's chest, she pleaded. "Move! Max, the bears are coming. Move Max, please."

Tears burned her eyes, the knowledge of her inevitable death striking home. Max wiped her tears, whispering soothing words as his strong hands bodily turned her around. He'd gone crazy. This had to be some ancient Indian ritual sacrifice of some kind. They had lulled her into loving them and now the bear God needed a not-so-virginal sacrifice.

Squeezing her eyes shut tight, she listened as the animals moved closer. The sound of their giant paws depressing into the snow with every step echoed in her ears. The click of their nails scratching against the wood planks of the porch sent her heart into overdrive. Closer, so much closer and Max wouldn't let her go, let her run.

Gillian needed to run. Run fast, and run far, and maybe they wouldn't catch her, eat her. The gentle breathing of the animals sounded so close, but she wouldn't open her eyes, wouldn't. Terror held her firmly in its grasp, refusing to let go. Her heart pounded in her chest, threatening to burst; her breathing came in short, shallow gasps.

"Gillian, open your eyes," Max murmured in her ear.

She whimpered and pressed back against him. Maybe if she pushed hard enough, she could go straight through him and get into the house—anything to get away from the humongous beasts in front of her.

The scent of hickory smoke and earth teased her nostrils, pulling memories from her mind, but she pushed them back. Now was not the time to remember her men, the men who had sacrificed her to bears. *Bears!*

A heated, wet tongue flicked the tips of her fingers on her right hand and she jerked to the left. When the action repeated on her left hand, she jerked to the right. The beasts were toying with her, playing games with their food before they devoured it. A tear leaked from beneath her lashes only to have it lapped away by one of the bears, starting a rushing torrent of tears. God, it had tasted her—probably to see if she was worth eating.

"Gilly, love, open your eyes," Max pleaded. His voice was a soothing, yet harsh whisper.

"No." She pushed the word past her tightened lips.

A cold, wet nose brushed the palm of her hand, moving it until her palm rested on the bear's muzzle. At least, she assumed it was his muzzle. Again, the other bear seemed to mirror the action until her hand rested on both of them.

"Just a little, Gilly. They won't hurt you. They just want to show you," Max begged again. Slitting her eyes, she met the gaze of one bear and then the other, their large black eyes staring at her so intently. Any second now they'd each be dining on hand tartar. "See. They won't hurt you, Gilly. Never you."

Max brushed his lips over her ear, pressing a kiss just below her earlobe. Damn the man for knowing about one of her "spots".

When the black bears rose to their feet and backed away from them, she did the same, pressing against Max. She begged him without words to move away, but he didn't listen. Instead, he held her fast, forcing her to remain still.

What happened next caused her heart to stop as she gasped for breath. *It couldn't be.* It wasn't natural. And yet, it took place before her eyes. If she hadn't watched it from beginning to end, she wouldn't have believed it herself.

A gray swirling mist wafted from beneath the bear's feet, twirling and twining around their limbs until the bears stood covered in the fog. Seconds ticked by as they were engulfed completely by the unnatural phenomenon until the great mist dissipated, receding back into the ground from whence it came, leaving… *Leaving two men in the bears' place?* Ronan and Conner knelt before her, shaking from the cold, but they were her men.

Max stepped aside, bringing her with him and allowing the naked Ronan and Conner to pass by them. They rushed through the door and Gillian, after wrenching free of Max's grasp, followed hot on their heels.

"What…" she yelled, grabbing their attention as they yanked on sweat pants. "Was that?"

Max slid his arms around her waist from behind, but she quickly sidestepped his embrace. *Hell, no.* She wouldn't give him that power again. "We thought it would be best to show you the truth about us, rather than try and tell you. We didn't think you'd be so scared."

Bringing a hand to her mouth, she kept her words bottled for a moment, afraid her fear would get the better of her and she'd say something she didn't truly mean. After a few moments, Gillian spoke. "After I nearly tore a hole through Conner to get home after seeing a bear near the river, what made you think this would be a better scenario?"

Conner had the grace to blush before answering. "Mom said the same thing."

"Well, your mother was right. Who would have thought that a woman who is married to three men as well as having raised three might know what she was talking about!" Gillian's voice rose as she spoke until she screamed the last word.

"We thought…" Ronan started, but his words died as Gillian slid down the wall, her legs unable to support her. The shock of seeing two bears and thinking she was about to be eaten by them had drained her of all energy. "God, Gilly!"

Gillian batted at the hands thrust toward her. She didn't want to be snuggled and hugged by them, she was too mad and she told them so. "Just because I can't stand and I need your help getting up doesn't mean you're forgiven. How dare you," she punched Ronan in the chest, "scare me like that? You ass. All of you are asses. I don't care if some great big fog comes up and changes you into bears, deep down, the fog didn't get it right and you're jackasses."

She allowed Ronan to gather her in his arms and didn't put up a fuss when he laid her gently on the bed in the spare bedroom.

When the three men moved to leave, she stopped them. "Oh no. You're staying and I'm getting answers. Now."

They froze in their tracks, each of them turning slowly to face her, a look of sheer terror painted on their faces. Good. Now they knew what it was like to be scared out of their minds.

Settling around her on the bed, they each proffered answers to her questions, sharing snippets of their tribe's history as well as the history of their family. They explained that their tribe consisted of all the Indians deemed "possessed" by the ancient tribes. Coming together, the men and women who held an animal within founded their own tribe, the Anikotas, which remained closely connected, even today. Now, scattered across the country, the people of the Anikota kept in touch through annual gatherings, but their tight bond held through their animal counterparts always remained. Their tribe didn't consist of only bears, but of every creature known to man. And each tribe member, whether man or woman, had a drive to find their mate unlike any other person they knew.

Their family, the Bearclaws, consisted of, well, bears. Typically, a Bearclaw wife gave birth to twins or triplets, and those siblings sought their one true mate to complete them—sometimes searching for years before finding their mate. The ability to transform from human to animal rested solely of those born into the Anikota tribe. But an Anikota mate, once the ritual of mating had been completed, could share the thoughts of their counterpart.

"And I'm your mate?" Gillian asked as they finished answering her other questions. She needed to know if her feelings were returned.

"Yes," they answered in unison, their voices blending and mixing into one.

"Are you ours?" Ronan, her deep, quiet, Ronan, asked the question, barely a whisper.

Gillian answered, just as softly, "Yes."

Chapter Thirteen

Ronan tensed as her admission washed through him. He could see his brothers had the same reaction. He knew what they felt as their bears woke from their slumber within and the spirits of man and beast warred for domination. Ronan had been trained by their fathers to guide the rite of claiming, to ensure the four of them survived and enjoyed the mating to come. A pre-determined sequence of events had to take place first. They would have to see to their mates needs before satisfying their own within her body.

As if on cue, Conner relinquished his position at her feet and the three of them shifted and changed places. The eldest at their mate's feet, the second eldest, Conner, to his right and the youngest, Max, to his left.

Ronan whispered the ancient words, so similar to those that allowed his change, yet different. He asked the Maker to bless their mating, to grant Gillian's womb to bear fruit and to grant their seed the power to join them. As the chant finished, his gaze met his sweet Gillian's.

"We're mating now, aren't we?" Curiosity and a hit of anticipation colored her voice.

"We are." He nodded. "Do you accept us, Gillian? Accept the three Bearclaw brothers as your mates in this life and all that follow?"

"Yes." She squirmed beneath his gaze, her knees pressed together as if trying to ease an ache. He'd ease it for her, they all would.

Grasping her ankles, Ronan removed one boot and then the next. Her socks quickly followed, as did her jeans and panties. As he worked on shedding the clothes on her lower half, Max and Conner worked on the upper half of her body. Soon, she lay naked before them.

"What about you?" Her bare foot slid against his cotton-covered thigh.

Ronan blushed, heat infused his cheeks before he rose from the bed and stripped, as did his brothers. They hadn't really planned mating right this moment with Gillian and it showed, but she didn't seem to mind. She lay passive; fingers trailing across her breasts, sliding lower to her delicate curls. Grasping her wrist, he stopped her from going further.

She poked out her lower lip. "Hey."

"Hey, yourself, Gilly." Crawling back between Gillian's raised knees, he waited for his brothers to join him, and noticed Max had remembered to grab the lube. *Thank God.* Ronan's thoughts so centered on tasting Gillian's sweet cream, he'd forgotten about his other duties to her.

Taking her hand in his, he slid it higher to rest on her breast. "Here or on them, but below the waist is mine for a while, Gilly."

Whimpering, she nodded and tweaked her nipple, gaze bouncing between Max and Conner. As much as he wanted to taste the sweet berries of her breasts, his job was to see all aspects of the mating went smoothly, including breaching the possibly virgin territory of Gilly's ass.

Ronan lowered his face to her golden hair-dusted mound and inhaled her scent—the sweet vanilla mint musk that'd drawn his attention the first day she ventured into their home. His cock ached and pulsed with the need to claim and mate with their Gillian.

Extending his tongue, he delved between her sodden folds, lapping at the tender skin and flesh beneath his mouth. Her taste exploded on his tongue, his beast scratching at the ethereal veil held in place by the Maker. Her musk intoxicated him as she writhed beneath his mouth. He lapped at her clit, sucking the bit of flesh and demanding her orgasm.

Bathing his fingers in her cream, he thrust two fingers into her heated passage. The snug fit strangling his digits with their strength as her muscles clamped down on the invasion. She screamed, her voice echoing against the wood plank walls of their home. His gaze traveled her body and he watched as she stroked his brothers, their heads thrown back as she pleasured them. Soon, soon they'd all feel the rapture of coming together as one.

Closing his eyes again, he focused on his task. Ensuring their mate was prepared for their joining had fallen to him and he would not fail. Adding droplets of lube to his fingers, he nudged her knees wider until his brothers helped him, grabbing a leg behind each knee and holding her open to him. Cunt and ass exposed to his questing hands, two fingers teased her puckered hole.

Gillian's back entrance clenched beneath his gentle probing, as if begging him to enter her quickly. His cock ached and pulsed in time with the tightening of her pussy and ass while his beast pressed against the veil. His fathers had warned him of this time when his control would be tested by the Maker. To fail would mean the death of those he loved most.

Sliding his fingers past the first ring of muscle, Gillian's muscles tensed, her legs nearly clamping around his head. Growling low enough for only his brothers to hear, he felt her legs widen in response. Good, they needed to focus on the ritual and not their own pleasure for now. Stretching Gillian's back entrance, he pushed his fingers further, her dark hole spreading and stretching to accommodate his invasion.

He pumped in and out of her pussy and ass in time with the suction he applied to her clit. They couldn't proceed without her orgasm, without offering her climax as a gift to the Maker. Curling the fingers in her pussy, he fluttered the tips along what he hoped were the bundle of nerves that would bring her orgasm to the surface. Gillian's hips rose from the bed, rocking and pressing harder to his face. Inhaling the scent of her increased musk, he darted his tongue to her core, lapping at the newest rush of cream bathing his fingers.

Gillian's screams and moans grew as his fingers and mouth worked her until finally her body tensed, freezing in mid-air, her cunt and ass tightening to the point of pain around his fingers as she released a guttural moan.

Her come bathed his fingers and his beast took a running leap at the veil. Squeezing his eyes shut, he fought the urge to change without the Maker's help and resisted the pull of the wild. Winning this first battle, he opened his eyes to see his brothers watching him warily.

Releasing Gillian's clit, he slid his fingers free of her body and rose to his knees, smiling to Conner and Max. They had passed the first phase of the mating. The heat of their woman had not pushed Ronan too far and now they were ready.

"Now, let us begin the mating." Ronan lifted a boneless Gillian into his arms, allowing his brothers to lie in their places.

*

"Begin?" They had to be kidding. Gillian was done already. The orgasm Ronan had wrenched from her had been the most powerful release of her life. *Begin?*

Ronan cradled her against his chest. She laid her head on his shoulder and listened to the beat of his heart, rapidly pulsing against her ear. He hadn't been unaffected. Eyes drifting closed, she allowed her men to position her as they desired, trusting they would care for her as they had for the past week and a half. When done, she lay chest to chest with Conner, knees on either side of his hips and his cock straining toward her pussy. Max knelt behind her with his cock nestled in the crack of her ass, while Ronan's strained inches from her face.

Ronan cupped her cheek, drawing her gaze from his shaft, up his body to his eyes. "We'll all love you together, Gilly."

Extending her tongue and shifting forward, she managed to capture a drop of his essence before he could stop her. Nature, pure and wild with a hint of hickory, burst on her tongue. Her men looked the same, but inside, they differed so greatly.

Max's cock, slick with cool lube, probed her back entrance, begging to be granted entry.

Whimpering, the pressure growing as he pressed forward, she looked to Ronan. "It's okay, Gilly, press out, let Max in. It'll feel so good, love, so good."

She did as he asked, she felt Max's width slide into her depths, stretching her wide, wakening nerves and sending the tingle of arousal coursing through her. Pressing back against Max, she eased more of his cock into her passage amid his groans and moans. More, she needed and wanted more of Max within her. When his groin met her backside, she whimpered. Gillian ached with the need to be filled further. Looking down into Conner's eyes, she imagined she'd get her wish.

A tap of her cheek brought her attention back to Ronan. "Now Conner, Gilly. He's going to fill you, stretch you so wide, but you'll love it." His thumb traced circles on her cheek.

At her nod she felt Conner's hand snake between them, skimming her chest, abdomen and lower belly before he moved his cock, poising it at her entrance. "Gotta move together, poppet. Ease on down, take me inside you."

Biting her lower lip, she stared into his eyes as she did as he asked. Lowering her body, rocking back onto his cock, she cried out at the feeling of being so filled. Her pussy felt as if it were ready to tear. "Conner…"

"Easy, Gilly, I've got you." His hand slid from his cock and his callused fingertips stroked her silken folds, strumming her clit to life. Her pussy clenched around his cock and she moved against her two men, taking Conner deeper. "That's it, Gilly. So hot, so tight."

His fingers played over her newly aroused nubbin, causing her cunt to ripple and tighten around Conner's welcome intrusion. Pressing her face to his neck, she rocked back and forth on Max and Conner's cocks, gasping with each withdrawal and surge forward. Her orgasm approached again, skittering along her spine with renewed fervor.

Ronan stroked her face, brushing the hair out of her eyes and capturing her attention again. "Slowly Conner. Our mate must come with us and not before."

"Spoil…" She gasped and whined as Conner slowed his magical fingers. "Sport." "Open for me, Gilly, take me in. We'll all come together when it's time; you need to bring us with you." Ronan ordered, a growl, deep and earthy had entered his voice as the tip of his cock probed her mouth.

Licking her lips, she opened for him, taking him deep with one giant suck. She wanted all her men had to give. Now. Rocking and shifting above Conner, she worked their cocks in and out of her body, tugging, sucking and tightening every hole they filled. Conner's hands twirled her aching clit, tapping it with each thrust backwards. Max stroked and skimmed her back, occasionally squeezing her ass when she tightened around him.

Trusting Conner and Max to guide her movements, she focused on giving Ronan pleasure. The man always held a tight control and she wanted to break, or at least bend, it a little. Flicking the underside of his cock with every suck, she licked the crown of his shaft, pressing her tongue into his slit before sliding down his shaft again. When the tip of his cock touched the back of her throat, she swallowed instinctively, taking him deeper into her mouth.

Back and forth. Back and forth. Over and over again she swallowed, thrust against and fucked her three men, her mates, urging them toward their orgasm even as she chased her own. It lingered at the edge of her consciousness, sliding along her spine, spreading from head to toe. The feelings of warmth enveloped her body and focused on her mates' point of entry. Her mouth, cunt and ass heated with each continued stroke. She increased her pace, working and begging for their release. Gillian ached to be filled by their seed.

Basking in their love, she listened as they began to chant in time with their lovemaking. Eyes drifting closed, the image of the three of them joined, loving one another, flitted through her mind. Their bodies became encased in the mystical fog, seeping into their pores, joining them in a way they never imagined.

As the fog in her mind receded, Gillian's orgasm burst forth, shooting through her, she screamed around Ronan's shaft. The feeling of shattering into a thousand pieces suddenly overtook her.

The dark taste of his seed spilled across her tongue and she drank from his cock as if drinking from a fountain. Every drop and pulse flowed freely down her throat. Max and Conner gripped her hips and the heated splash of their release flooded into her passages. They'd come together, sharing in the intimate release as one.

Licking and sucking the last bit of Ronan's come from his deflating erection, Gillian reluctantly released him, easing him from her mouth. Max withdrew from her ass in slow, aching movements, leaving her empty. Last was Conner. He slid her to his side, holding and petting her as he slid his cock free of her pussy. Tired, aching, she drifted to sleep, her men, her mates, surrounding her.

Minutes or hours later, Gillian awoke to her mates crowded around her, staring at her chest. "I know my breasts are great, guys, but they're not all that."

She chuckled at her own joke, shivering when Ronan traced a circle above her left breast. "You belong to us now, Gilly."

Smiling, she cupped Ronan's cheek. "I know, love, I know."

"No," he affirmed. "You are ours. The Maker has blessed our union." He stroked her breast again.

Following his finger, she found a mark that hadn't been there before. Above her left breast a midnight black tattoo of a bear's paw had appeared as she slept.

Staring from one brother to the next, she found tears brimming, threatening to spill at any moment. She wished she could hug them all at once, but the best she could do was love them.

"I am yours. Forever."

The End

ABOUT CELIA KYLE

Ex-dance teacher, former accountant and erstwhile collectible doll salesperson, New York Times and USA Today bestselling author Celia Kyle now writes paranormal romances for readers who:

1) Like super hunky heroes (they generally get furry)

2) Dig beautiful women (who have a few more curves than the average lady)

3) Love laughing in (and out of) bed.

It goes without saying that there's always a happily-ever-after for her characters, even if there are a few road bumps along the way.

Today she lives in central Florida and writes full-time with the support of her loving husband and two finicky cats.

If you'd like to be notified of new releases, special sales, and get FREE ebooks, subscribe here: http://celiakyle.com/news

You can find Celia online at:

http://celiakyle.com
http://facebook.com/authorceliakyle
http://twitter.com/celiakyle

COPYRIGHT

Published by Summerhouse Publishing. Battered Not Broken. Copyright © 2014 Celia Kyle. ALL RIGHTS RESERVED. This book contains material protected under International and Federal Copyright Laws and Treaties. Any unauthorized reprint or use of this material is prohibited. No part of this book may be reproduced or transmitted in any form or by any means, electronic or mechanical, including photocopying, recording, or by any information storage and retrieval system without express written permission from the author.

This is a work of fiction. The characters, incidents and dialogues in this book are of the author's imagination and are not to be construed as real. Any resemblance to actual events or persons, living or dead, is completely coincidental.

CPSIA information can be obtained
at www.ICGtesting.com
Printed in the USA
LVHW090756120222
710986LV00019B/509